THE HAUNTING OF ASPENDALE MANOR

KENNA BELLRAE

This publication is a work of fiction. All names, descriptions, dates, places, and events are imaginary and any likeness or correlation to real-world circumstances is purely coincidental.

Copyright © 2024 Kenna Bellrae

All rights reserved.
No part of this book may be reproduced or used in any manner without the prior written permission of the copyright owner, except for the use of brief quotations in a book review or discussion.
To request permissions, contact authorkennabellrae@gmail.com

First paperback edition November 2024.
Edited by Norma Gambini

One for sorrow,
Two for joy,
Three for a girl,
Four for a boy,
Five for silver,
Six for gold,
Seven for a secret never to be told.
Eight for a wish,
Nine for a kiss,
Ten a surprise you should be careful not to miss,
Eleven for health,
Twelve for wealth,
Thirteen beware it's the devil himself.
("One For Sorrow," nursery rhyme)

TRIGGER WARNING

Asylum, barbaric psychiatry mentioned, blood play, breath play, breeding kink, gore, knife play, mental health, mental illness, murder, mention of suicide, mention of torture, psychiatric treatment facility, unprotected sex, use of safeword.

ONE
THE MACABRE MANSION AND THE INSCRUTABLE TENANT

BLAIR

"BLAIR, *this is what you've always wanted, holy shit!*"

My best friend, Iris's, words echoed in my mind as I approached Aspendale Manor. Its appearance was striking and my stomach twisted, but overall, I was ecstatic.

Dr. Norman Aspendale studied the criminally insane, was fascinated with mental illness specifically regarding abhorrent individuals and their behavior. He'd taught a special summer class during my final year in college, and I'd been thrilled to learn he'd planned to open an internship for new assistants. He'd been looking for two, and the application process had been rigorous enough to weed out would-be skeptics. Overall, twelve were chosen.

The manor had been in Dr. Aspendale's family for centuries. He was a legacy himself, his family an even larger one. They were all notable psychiatrists with their own innovative discoveries in the field. The manor carried a dark and disturbing history, especially early on in its founding, and as a result the haunted rumor mill was never lacking. It was said that the wings branching from the main house had been home to some of the country's most dangerous and mentally ill prisoners.

That practice had died out decades ago, and the majority of the manor sat empty now. But still, it was enough to question if such a haunting was present.

Working for Dr. Aspendale as a mere assistant wasn't the long-term goal by any stretch of the imagination. Some would say that viewing him as a steppingstone was callous, but with no children of his own, the manor and his practice wouldn't continue without a protégé. My hope was that walking away with an assistant position would grant me the opportunity to take over. I'd spent the first couple years in college wondering what I wanted to do, but I'd quickly fallen in love with forensic psychology and the endless possibilities. Since that day, it'd felt like everything had aligned perfectly for this moment.

The manor's haunted claims did little to deter me from the opportunity; I'd never been a believer. Skeptic seemed too harsh, but I was a woman of science and evidence. Too many times over, evidence had been fabricated, and how disappointing that was. The mere idea of a supernatural plane perfectly aligned with ours was exciting to imagine. I supposed that was where it stopped for me, just a wish.

The black sedan stopped, and I looked at the driver in the rearview mirror. He was part of the Aspendale staff and had been tasked with picking me up from the airport. He was stoic and quiet; I'd never even gotten a name, much less a greeting.

"Thank you," I said quietly, expecting his returned silence. As I stepped out, so did he, quick to remove my bags from the trunk.

The manor was intimidating as I gazed upon it, like an ant to a giant. The stone was old, some of it original and some of it newly reconstructed. Vines and other greenery grew along the rough, brick structure. From the outside, it looked like there were at least four floors, but its design made it hard to discern for sure. Spires sat atop towers, and it was every Victorian era lover's dream property. A fountain and shrubbery decorated the expansive front lawn alongside marble statues.

Picture-perfect creepy.

I looked around, but the car and its driver had gone, leaving me with the giant bags. Turning around, I was startled as a young woman stood in front of me. I hadn't heard her approach on the gravel walkway. She was thin, small in frame, and wore a well-fitting gray suit. Her hair was a golden blonde color, but it was slicked back into a tight French twist. Makeup was minimal, but she looked ethereal.

"Blair Grimm," she said, her voice gentle and as light as she.

"Yes, ma'am."

"I'm Cressida Clairmont, Dr. Aspendale's personal assistant and secretary." I thought over her words. She wasn't one of his interns or psychology assistants by that description. "Your room will be in the east wing on the third floor. It's the first room." She turned, her steps silent as she approached the manor. I looked after her in awe before shaking my head and gathering my bags.

They were heavy and loud as I dragged them behind me. It was a struggle to keep them moving together and myself upright. Stepping inside, I spied that the lobby was empty except for Cressida. Her hand was outstretched with a simple key as I approached. She pointed to the right, and there the labeled entrance sat for the east wing. I turned to thank her, but she was gone. No steps, no closing of doors, it was like she'd evaporated into thin air.

I shoved the key into my pocket and lugged my entire life into the untrustworthy east wing elevator. It was slow and noisy. By its appearance, I wondered if this thing had claimed any lives.

The gate opened, revealing a floor with two doors, one at the beginning of the hall and one at the end. There was a scent to the air, but it was hard to discern the notes. I appreciated the security of a locked room as I watched the second door swing open. As I unlocked mine, the scent of tobacco was stronger behind the door, and I looked back to the second room. He was . . . consuming. The way he held himself gave a sense of confidence, not arrogance, and his physical attractiveness supported that as he leaned against the frame. I didn't know who he was, but he could easily be a problem. My face flushed under his piercing blue gaze.

Beyond a polite observance time, I blinked and walked across the threshold. The image of the white-blond man leaning against his doorframe was sure to be seared into my mind. He was almost too tall to fit inside it, and his crossed arms and sly grin all but screamed trouble.

I wasn't here for trouble.

Or distractions.

HEATH

MY DOOR WAS CRACKED open the slightest bit, but even if it hadn't been, the elevator creaking its way up was loud enough to have me listening for footsteps. It was early in the evening, but late enough that I had questioned if my floor companion would show up at all.

The sound of plastic wheels on hardwood complemented her heels. I stood quickly, opening my door and taking pause. I'd intended to say hello, or at least a polite greeting, but I stopped there in the doorframe. Transfixed entirely.

Her hair was dark and it fell in long waves down her back. The sides were slicked back with striking silver pins. Every inch of her was beautiful. The upturned and sharp nose, the dark brows and framing lashes. She wasn't very tall, even in heels. Her posture was nearly perfect.

Delicate hands gripped and pushed obnoxiously large suitcases into the room. She stood straight and looked back at mine, noticing I stood there now. Her eyes widened a fraction before she looked me up and down, disappearing with nothing more for me.

Now, she is the most interesting person I've seen so far.

The metallic click of her lock sent me back to my suite. I picked up my phone from the desk and looked through the email sent to us regarding the internship acceptance. I scrolled down and read over the applicants and their room assignments.

East wing, third floor, Blair Grimm.

Beautiful.

I grabbed a fresh notebook from my bag. She didn't belong in a notebook filled with the mundane. Her study would be of its own, how it deserved to be.

On a fresh page, I scrawled her name at the top and sketched her from memory. The pose was how she'd stood to unlock the door. From there, I drew her hands in their own study. Her fingers were long and thin, and her nails were sharp. A vintage ring sat on her middle finger.

I looked up from the sketch pad, noting it was time for dinner. Time had passed for her to settle in, and I hoped that she'd be up for walking with me down to the main floor. I replaced the notebook as the clock tower on the grounds chimed seven times. I left my door open, and I heard the faintest sound of her lock disengaging. On quick but quiet steps, I approached just as she walked out. Her hand went to her chest, as if she were startled as she touched the silver chain that sat over her black turtleneck sweater.

"Dinner?" I asked like we were casual friends as I produced a clean crow's feather. She only nodded, taking the feather and twirling it in her fingers. I kept talking, hoping to hear her voice at some point tonight. "I'll walk you down, if that's okay?"

"Sure," she said, husky and deeper than one would expect based on her appearance. She locked her room, and I held out my arm. She hesitantly took my elbow in her hand.

"Heath Crowley, by the way." She looked up at me with a polite but awkward smile.

"Blair Grimm."

"Blair," I said sweetly. "It's nice to meet you. Where'd you study at?"

"Radcliffe University." Her answers were short.

Conversation didn't seem to be too high on her list for today . . . or at all.

"East Coast, right?"

"Yes, up north." I led her down the stairwell. She twirled the crow's feather faster with anxious and cautious steps.

"They had you carry all that luggage up these stairs by yourself?" She looked up at me, her brows scrunched quizzically. She knew I'd heard the elevator.

"It really wasn't that much trouble, considering the elevator." I laughed at her subtle call out of my poor attempt to keep the conversation going.

"All the same, I wish I'd been at the main house when you arrived. I would've helped." She shook her head, looking away from me. "Have you met any of the other interns?"

"No, you're the first." I wasn't sure how to take that. Her tone was indifferent, and I was certain she didn't care to make friends while she was here.

"Flattered, really. I have a proposition for you." I stopped as we reached the first floor and the annex for the main house. My hand rested at her elbow as I turned her toward me.

"A proposition?" Her eyebrow raised, dark and perfectly arched. I started to speak, but people suddenly filled the space and I dropped the topic and her arm. "Later," I said, bending down to her ear as she straightened. "Stop by my suite after dinner and we can talk." When I looked into those beautiful brown eyes again, I plastered my smile on. "Lovely chat, thank you for walking with me, Ms. Blair."

I held out my hand and it dwarfed hers, but the touch was light and soft.

"Thank you for the offer," she said with a healthy dose of skepticism as she looked me up and down again. I took it as a win nonetheless and turned for the dining hall.

Little Blair, you and I will be great partners.

TWO
DROWNING IN BLOOD

BLAIR

I DISCARDED my dishes and looked around the dining hall. I hadn't seen Heath again after I'd found a secluded place to eat. His proposition wasn't real yet left me stumped, and I was hopeful he'd try to tell me again so I didn't have to visit his room. Unfortunately, that wasn't the case, and I found myself moving through the doors and halls, on my way up the stairs and straight to him. I wanted to ask about the feather. What could a gift like that mean? Was it an omen? Why did I care?

I walked quietly down the hall. His door was open, and I stopped just before the threshold. I debated, going back and forth in my mind on whether this was going to be some cruel act instead. If I entertained the idea and got burned in return—

"Come in, Ms. Blair."

His voice sliced through my thoughts and urged me forward. Inside, I turned and observed his room, a mirror to mine. It smelled familiar, but that was impossible. His back was to me as he sat at an exact replica of my desk. He stood and closed a notebook before clearing the top of it completely.

"Have a seat," he said, stepping away and gesturing to his chair. I took measured steps across the room and sat, but his hands fell to the backrest and pushed me across the room toward his bed. He sat in front of me on the firm mattress.

We stared at each other for a beat; I was sure I gave off panic and mistrust.

"Enjoy dinner?" His attempt at breaking the tension.

"I did." My failure to maintain the broken tension. As I spun the feather out of nervous habit, I watched the dark blues and blacks catch the dying light through his window. He was friendly, but he was still a mystery, and it'd benefit me to have walls in place. So far, my only real observation was his general attractiveness. I knew nothing about him.

"My proposition," he started immediately. "Let's be partners."

"Partners?"

"Everyone is under the impression it's a competition between all twelve, but it doesn't have to be. Teamwork is important to Dr. Aspendale."

"I'm aware." What he said made sense, and it was a fact, but his choice of me was what I couldn't wrap my head around.

"While they're keeping secrets and working against each other, we can push each other forward."

"And you've decided I'm the perfect partner because?"

"You're insanely smart, Blair. Radcliffe is a prestigious institution for psychology." I didn't need to be flattered.

"I'm sure there are others just as intelligent here." He grinned, one side of his mouth tilting upward. It was hypnotizing. He spoke with charm. His demeanor was inviting, and slowly he started to weave a spell over me. He knew of his effect.

"Unfortunately for them, I saw you first." It was a weird thing to claim, but I didn't entirely hate it. I almost liked his attention if I had to admit it. I crossed my arms and studied him. It was a decent offer. He seemed pleasant to be around, which would be a plus.

"And if I say yes, are you going to make me do everything while you benefit?" He laughed—it was airy and light and bordered on insulting. Though, the melodic sound was attractive.

"Absolutely not. I have talents of my own to bring to the table." I leaned forward and he mirrored me. Entirely too close, but neither of us corrected it. My chest started to warm, and I hoped it wouldn't creep to my cheeks. I noticed then the scent wasn't from his room; it was from him. Fainter still, but the same.

"What talents might those be?"

"Find out, Ms. Blair." He dared me, and I was foolish enough to take it. Call it curiosity or falling for the lure of his charm.

"Alright," I said, leaning back and spinning to take in his room again. Really, I needed to be out of his bubble. The air was becoming thick. "I don't see why not. I'd be willing to give it a chance. With conditions, of course." My world spun as he turned me to face him. My breathing picked up. *No distractions,* I told myself. Any form of distance I put between us was disrupted by his advances.

"What are they?"

"If I don't like you or if I feel like our deal is very one-sided, then I walk and you don't approach me about the topic again." I realized too late that it sounded like he could approach me about anything else, but I didn't take the opportunity to correct that miscommunication. And I didn't know that I wanted to.

"That sounds perfect," he said, holding out his hand for mine. The gentle way he'd held my hand on the way to dinner came back to me as I slid my palm against his. His touch sent a shiver down my spine.

A chill filled the air then. From the corner of my eye, I saw the door move slightly, but before I could look over, it slammed. I jumped, gripping his hand harder, but he didn't complain.

"Do you believe in ghosts, Blair?" he asked when I looked at him again.

"I don't." I looked at our joined hands and quickly released him as my cheeks blushed. Sitting back in his chair and crossing my arms, I hoped he didn't notice.

"Unfortunate, because the manor is haunted and they definitely believe in you."

"Those are silly claims," I said, waving him off and dismissing any notions of a haunting. It had been the wind.

"I wouldn't be so sure. The east and west wings housed special patients in the past." I stood, walking away from him and to his desk. The sound of my heels filled his dead-quiet room. When I looked over my shoulder, I noticed his gaze was glued to my feet as I walked.

"Though true," I said, trailing off to sit atop the end of his desk facing the window. I pointed, indicating that it was indeed open. He stood behind me, just off to my side as he peered beyond my hand. "The main estate was for family and employees. The Aspendale Asylum was at the back of the property and had a separate entrance. They didn't keep patients here."

I looked over my shoulder and up at him. His eyes were distant before he glanced down at me.

"How sure are you of that?" His hand planted on the desk at my far side, too close once again, and I found myself warming inside.

"I've done my research and read the documents that were public."

He nodded and asked, "But not the private ones?"

"You have?"

"I've read many things one probably shouldn't have."

That felt oddly like flirting, and I didn't know what to do with that yet. I looked over his shoulder, noting the door was open again. His movement distracted me from my line of questioning as he produced his phone with an empty contact page pulled up. He handed it to me.

I typed in the necessary details and sent myself a message with his name. He stopped me before I could hand it back to him.

"Picture." He nodded to the phone, but I raised an eyebrow at him. "What if I confuse you with someone else?"

"Do you know another Blair?"

"Thankfully, just the one." His voice was husky, and I was sure then he'd been flirting, and though I didn't want to give in so easily, my body betrayed me as I smirked and blushed at the statement. His attention posed to be a lethal weapon with the wrong intentions.

I acquiesced, holding the phone up to snap a quick photo. I didn't smile, but that didn't stop Heath from moving into frame and doing so. His chest brushed against my back and my breath hitched.

Setting the phone on his desk, I gently pushed on his chest until he backed away from my personal space and I slid off the top. He let me walk across the room without a word, and at the threshold, I felt that chill once more. When I looked back, his eyes were on my heels again. I held onto the doorframe as I watched his gaze slowly move to meet mine. He sat against the edge of the desk with his arms crossed.

"Good night, Heath." He said nothing still, letting me walk out and to my room.

LATE INTO THE NIGHT, after studying and preparing for the next day, I put away my things and started the shower. The pipes were old, and I let the water run for a minute to warm up. A smokey and earthy scent settled in the bathroom, similar to what I'd smelled when I'd first arrived. *Odd.*

The coming weeks were promising, even more so if Heath's proposition panned out. I stepped inside once it steamed. The hot water washed over my body and eased the stress in my shoulders. The gentle pressure of the shower slipped me into a thoughtful trance.

With Dr. Aspendale choosing two assistants, it was likely that they'd be the top two performers during this internship. If Heath's proposal were all it was cracked up to be, we'd probably end up working together if we put ourselves on top. I didn't know how I felt about that. There was an odd attraction I hadn't parsed out yet. Part of me fought against it, but another part of me was on board completely.

The slam of my door scared me and I jumped, nearly slipping on the soapy tub floor. I'd locked it when I'd gotten back from my meeting with Heath. There was no wind to close anything.

"Hello?" As I expected, nothing and no one answered me. I reached out and dried my hands on a towel before grabbing my phone.

> Blair: Did you come into my room?

Heath: No?

I didn't explain further, content that it wasn't my door I'd heard but his. Or even the door to the stairwell. I'd locked mine. I was sure and certain of myself. Rinsing my hair, I let that worry wash down the drain. The supernatural wasn't real, and the ghosts of Aspendale Manor weren't either.

Floorboards creaked and I stopped. My imagination was playing tricks on me again and I'd prove it, *again*. I waited for the sound of more, but none came. A satisfied smile settled on my lips as I closed my eyes.

"Blair?"

I gasped and pulled back the curtain, peeking out to see Heath standing in the bathroom doorway.

"You scared the shit out of me!" But, Heath *stood* there.... "How did you even get into my suite?"

"Your door was open," he said so confidently, as though I were the stupid one here.

"No, I closed it and locked it."

"Ready to believe in ghosts yet?" He smirked and I rolled my eyes, suddenly aware of the situation. I closed the curtain with a sharp flick of my wrist.

"So funny. Thank you for coming to check on me; can you close the door on your way out?" I heard his feet shuffle on the hardwood and in delusion, I thought I heard him respond.

"Anything for you, dear."

I looked through the curtain toward the door. It closed and I breathed in peace once again. Finished, I stepped out and wrapped a towel around myself. I ran to the door immediately and ensured it was locked.

I dressed and set my alarm, wasting no time and not giving Heath another chance to rescue me from nothing.

I WOKE UP NATURALLY, rubbing my eyes. My blurred vision cleared and I saw Heath standing at the foot of my bed. "How did you get in here?" I wiped my eyes again, sure I was hallucinating and the man wasn't stupid enough to intrude on my space for no reason in this manner. Only, when I looked again, I wasn't in my room. I was in the main house annex.

Weird.

So fucking weird.

"Good morning." I turned around, seeing the same pretty white-blond hair and piercing blue eyes from last night.

"Heath," I said. It sounded more like a question, and he nodded like he didn't understand my confusion. "Were you in my room this morning?"

"No," he said, his tone overly flirtatious and not at all like what I'd heard from him just yesterday. "But I wish I had been."

His arms wrapped around my waist, but I hardly felt the contact as I tried to wrap my head around the action. My mind couldn't keep up with any of it, especially when he moved to kiss me. It was hollow, his contact nothing but emptiness and just a motion.

He pulled back and looked down at me in pain. Blood pooled in his mouth and dripped over his lips.

A line of blood appeared on his throat from nowhere, a silent plea escaping his lips as it dripped and stained his white shirt.

"Heath?" He dropped, falling into my arms like a weightless feather. It should've been harder to hold him up. He was heavier than I was. He coughed, but it came out like a strained gurgle. "Heath? Help! Somebody help, please!"

The blood continued to pour from him, flowing over my fingers and staining my hands red. There was so much. So much more than what any adult body would typically hold. I closed my eyes, screaming.

"Somebody help him!"

"BLAIR!" My eyes flew open in a panic and I pushed myself up, feeling a cool hand on the side of my face. I focused thanks to an oil lamp's little bit of light in my room. The white-blond hair took shape then. "Hey, there," Heath said more casually, but there was a layer of fear or concern laced through it.

I reached out, not caring about appropriateness. I

needed to know he was real. He was solid beneath my touch. My hands moved to both sides of his face, skimming over his cheeks. My fingers traced his lips, *no blood*. My fingers traced his throat, *no blood*.

"As much as I appreciate the contact," he started, grabbing my wrists in his hands. "Can I ask what you're looking for?" He laughed, but he didn't release me.

"I-I'm sorry. It was a dream."

"That would explain why you were screaming my name like bloody murder," he said, nodding and piecing together things I couldn't. I hadn't even screamed his name in my dream. I'd just wanted help.

"I did? Are you sure?" My heart raced and sent me into a panicked panting.

"You did, yeah. What happened?" Heath released my wrists then, sliding a thumb across my cheek as he settled onto my bed fully.

"I saw you by the bed. And then we were doing something for Dr. Aspendale, a-and you . . ." I looked at him and then over his shoulder, noting the wide open door. In that moment, some clarity hit and I decided it best to keep the kiss my little secret.

His hand under my chin guided my focus back to him. "I what, Blair?"

"You were there and then blood, so much blood." I felt my heart surge and my stomach drop.

"Do you normally have night terrors?" I shook my head, but he stilled the motion with his hands. "I'm very much alive and real."

He took my trembling hand and dragged it over his face, down his neck, and onto his chest right over his heart. I felt it then, the *thump-thump* beating that confirmed his statement.

"See? Alive and well, as best as the rest of us."

"I'm so sorry." I felt silly. I'd never had night terrors before, and embarrassment flushed my face.

"For?"

"Waking you up?" I wasn't sure and I was second-guessing myself. I felt apologetic, burdensome. The last thing I intended to be was his disruptive floormate.

He simply shrugged. "I was already awake. Sweet of you to care about your new partner though," he said, smirking. He held me and the tight grip of his fingers in my hair kept me grounded in reality.

He stood fully after a beat, and he was dressed down in his pajamas, just sweatpants with an exposed V line. I wondered if he'd been honest about being awake or if I'd woken him up and he didn't want me to feel bad. All the same, I did. I looked down at my lap as shame filled me. Another gentle pull of my focus put my eyes back on his.

"It's fine, I promise. Get some sleep, okay?" I nodded, but I couldn't promise anything. "Down the hall if you need me, door's open. Definitely call out if you see a ghost."

I couldn't help but laugh at the silly remark. Ghosts weren't real, and I shook my head from his hand, looking down at the floor. There was a feather-soft touch on my hair. The gentlest kiss I'd ever received. He walked to my door, and I was scared to look up. Even though it had only been a dream . . .

"Goodnight, Blair," was all he said before disappearing down the hall and to his room.

I lay back on my pillows and stared at the ceiling. Sleep took me eventually, but I didn't dream again the entire night.

THREE
RESTLESS RECORDS

BLAIR

THE MORNING WAS UNEVENTFUL. As I dressed, I decided to chalk everything up to extreme stress over recent travel and what was to come from the internship. Knowing myself, when I locked the door this time, I recorded it on my phone. I wasn't crazy thinking I had. It was a form of security. It was intentional, and I knew I did it every time.

I looked down the hall but was met with a different sight. Heath's door was closed. Down the stairs and in the main house, I skipped a full breakfast and opted for a quick snack from the pantry for later. The daily task board sat in the annex and was hard to miss. Wire letter baskets were marked with our names; finding mine, I snatched the sealed envelope from it.

"Morning!" The chipper voice beside me didn't belong to Heath, and I didn't have time to wonder why that disappointed me. I looked over, recognizing a woman from last night's dinner, but I hadn't talked to her.

"You're Blair, right?" She pointed to the basket. "I'm Clarice. It's nice to meet you."

"You, too," I said, cautiously and uncertain of her sudden interest in me.

"I'm staying in the west wing; what about you?" She was far too much like sunshine this early in the morning.

"East," I said, pointing over my shoulder.

"A lot of these people must be early risers," she mused, gazing at the board with hands on her hips. I looked over the task board with her, noting that many of the envelopes had been retrieved before my arrival.

An all too familiar hand reached over my shoulder, snatching one up. "Good morning," Heath said, his low voice in my ear startling, as it took me back to my nightmare.

"Hi, I'm Clarice!"

"Heath," he said simply, but he didn't look at her as I turned around. He was eyeing me, but Clarice was beyond noticing as she moved from person to person, striking up conversation wherever she could for however long.

I stepped away, knowing Heath would follow me. As I turned over the envelope, a firm hand pressed into the small of my back. "Hey, you okay?" We stopped in the corner of the annex, waiting for Cressida to greet us.

"Just unpleasant dreams and all," I said, looking up at him. I watched his throat, looking for the pulse of his artery.

"I see," he whispered before squeezing my hand. "Alive and well."

I nodded, repeating him. "Alive and well."

Looking around the room, I counted absentmindedly. Then, I counted again. Eleven. Including myself, there were only eleven people in the annex. I looked over at the task board, noting one envelope still in its basket, unclaimed.

Not a good way to start.

"Good morning, interns! We met as you all arrived, but once again, I am Cressida Price, Dr. Aspendale's secretary. You each have your daily task, and you will receive a new one every day. Your completion process is your own to determine, but all tasks are to be completed by the end of the week for consideration."

I felt Heath bump my elbow, and when I looked up, he winked. *Partners,* he silently reminded me.

"That's all for the morning brief; mind the schedule for main house operations, but you are free to get started on your work." Cressida walked away, and people started leaving by themselves in pairs, and even small groups. Chatty Clarice left with one of the groups, thankfully.

"Ready to give this a try?" Heath asked, holding up his envelope.

"Yeah," I said, swallowing hard around the word.

"What's wrong?" I looked at the board, not knowing why I cared so much about it.

"Someone didn't show up."

"Less competition," he said nonchalantly, shrugging it off. He opened his envelope and sat on one of the sofa chairs. I followed, but I didn't sit. Reading my assignment, I inwardly groaned. I had to do a report on a case study.

"What's your first task?"

"What's yours?" I countered.

"Someone's suspicious," he teased. "Archives. Dr. Aspendale wants to see my proposed improvement plan for record retention utilizing skills earned from my education program." He handed me the paper. He wasn't lying.

"I worked in a records department for an inpatient facility while I was at Radcliffe," I said. "I have to do a case study."

"To the records we go. We can pull your file while I work on a new plan."

"That simple?"

"Only for you," he said, smiling again before standing and offering his arm. "Shall we?" I wrapped my fingers around the crook of his elbow and silently followed him. I looked back once more at the abandoned letter before dropping the topic for good.

"This place is—"

"Abysmal?" he finishes, cutting me off.

"Something like that," I agreed. The records room was large with filing cabinets a head taller than me, but more than that—it was in complete disarray. It was no wonder why this was the first task. It'd be beneficial to no one in that state. "Dr. Aspendale is a mad man," I muttered under my breath.

"First," Heath said, taking the envelope from my

hand. I walked through the maze of files, finding an empty spot at a round table. "Let's get your patient." He opened my letter and read it off. "Name is Charlotte Van. She was admitted—"

He stopped abruptly and, after the shuffling of feet, reached for a a dark blue file folder, dropping in front of me.

"How did you find that so quickly?"

"On top of the first cabinet, believe it or not," he said, grinning and quietly boasting about his swiftness.

"I wouldn't have found that, thank you." The folder was thick and heavy as I picked it up and rifled through its contents.

"Lucky I'm here then," he teased, and I shook my head, not deigning to entertain him further.

I pulled my laptop from my bag, grateful that we'd decided to go back for anything we couldn't relocate down here. I started with the earliest date of patient notes, quietly reading and writing down anything important that stood out to me. Heath rummaged through files around me. He started with compiling and returning them to their current system.

"I think I might work on the actual system tomorrow; I can't think in such a pigsty," he grumbled as he walked past me with another stack of folders. "If I get the other assistant position with you, I'm going to give him hell for this level of disorder."

"You do that," I mumbled under my breath. My focus returned fully to correcting this patient's chart. There was no clear indication on which diagnosis and when from Dr. Aspendale, but starting at the beginning would ensure I was on the right track. There were clear errors from the first page, and I resigned myself to the fact that this was going to take most of the week to manage.

I'd never felt so drained and bored with a case study prior to Charlotte Van's. Energy left me as I flipped through each page, and I just wanted to nap. My eyes blurred the words as they closed and I slumped forward.

"Blair." The whisper of my name reached me with the shaking of my shoulder. "You okay?" I blinked tired eyes open through a foggy and slow mind.

"What?" I said, yawning.

"I asked if you're okay," Heath repeated. "You've been asleep for almost two hours. At first, I thought you were tired and needed a quick nap, but you weren't waking up on your own." I yawned again.

What the hell?

I looked around the room; the original mess had been cleaned up and there was a single filing cabinet strewn about.

"New system starts tomorrow." His words pulled my gaze back to him. "Hey, seriously, are you feeling okay? You look really pale." The back of his hand rested on my forehead and then my cheek before moving to my neck.

"I'm just . . ." I looked back to my laptop, but it was dead. Movement around the filing cabinets caught my attention.

"It's just you and me here, Grimm."

"But there's . . ." I caught the shadowy apparition moving through the row. Standing, I knocked the chair over. Unease urged me to flee.

"Hey, hey, talk to me."

"Th-there's—"

Strong fingers pulled at my chin and gripped my jaw, pinning my eyes to him. "Talk *to* me."

"It was a dark thing. I don't know." I couldn't shake my head—his grip didn't allow for much movement.

"Don't look around, but can you still see it?" His face filled most of my view, but just on the edge I saw the darkness creep and move. "Yes, my left." He released me, taking my hands instead and running us out of the records room. My eyes widened when the mass moved with us.

"It's beside you," I whispered.

"It's fine, stay with me." I shut my eyes, trusting him to lead me. The darkness had crept over his shoulders and I didn't want to see it anymore.

A door closed, and I presumed we were in the hall now, but I refused to look, not when it would mean seeing him cloaked in *that*. Heath's hand cupped the back of my head and pressed me to his chest.

"Is it still here?" I muttered into his shirt.

"You tell me." His voice hummed through his chest, and I chanced a peek. No shadows. No sweeping darkness around his body. I looked up at him, but he was already grinning down at me. Heath was every bit relaxed and collected.

"It's gone," I confirmed. The smile creeping onto my face stopped short as the doorknob clicked and tried to turn.

"How about we go back to our wing? You can get ready for lunch, I'll bring your file upstairs—minus the spirit—and we can spend the day there," he said, walking me down the corridor.

"But you need to do the files," I started, but I

stopped myself from looking back to the records room.

"That can wait," he assured me. "You're shaking like a leaf, Blair. This is more important."

Before he could take us too far away, I stilled my nerves and chanced a look back.

The doorknob still tried to turn.

FOUR
READY TO BELIEVE?

HEATH

I CLOSED HER DOOR GENTLY; she was rattled enough, and I didn't want to startle her with a loud and inconsiderate bang. I took the notebook from my pocket and flipped to a mostly clean page. After talking to her about it, I jotted down the important information, like her allergy and preferred coffee.

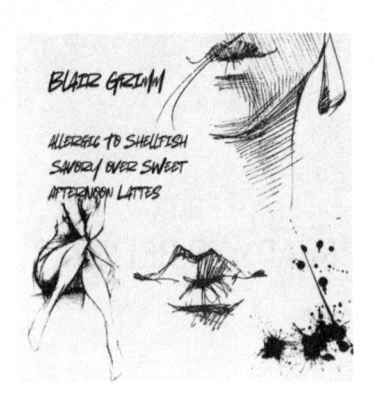

Down the hall, my suite was open, and I stepped inside to discard the notebook on my desk. Rifling through a drawer, I located an extra bundle of rosemary and herbs. *The sooner she accepts the supernatural, the better we'll be able to handle it.* I stopped my own train of thought because really, I wanted her to be able to protect herself. If she remained ignorant to what was attaching itself to her, then she'd never be able to stop it and . . . I didn't want to verbalize what the consequences could be.

Leaving my suite, I made my highest priority the records room. I hadn't seen what had been tormenting Blair, but I'd felt it. I'd felt her terror, too.

The way she'd clung to me, a stranger turned reluctant ally and not yet friend, she'd been genuinely afraid. Stopping in the hall before the door, I prepped the herbal bundle and let its smoke and scent wash over me and down the hall. Fear wasn't exactly the emotion that crept up inside me. It was a mixture. I couldn't see this thing; I couldn't see anything that Blair could, but I could feel it and that left me with uncertainty and terror.

I wanted to know what this was, yet I wasn't thrilled to find out by myself.

By now, the doorknob had stopped moving on its own, and I let myself inside. The disarray was how I'd left it and nothing new was out of place. Though the rosemary was calming, the energy in the room was anything but. I walked in a maze-like pattern through the filing cabinets and storage shelves.

"I don't appreciate you terrorizing my friend like that. She's a very sweet person just trying to do her job." I made it to the row she first spotted it in. "Her energy wasn't yours to take. You need to leave, and don't bother my friend again." The energy was palpable and I followed it, pushing it back further.

When I reached the door and effectively pushed it out, the room changed. Everything was lighter. I wanted to enjoy the feeling, but I knew it wasn't likely to last. I decided to leave my mess as it was and collect her things. I had plenty of time to waste today running through my ideas on paper and researching systems Aspendale would find favorable.

In the main house, the kitchen staff had prepared lunches rolling out. They sat in warm cases, and I hoped she'd like whatever I found. I really didn't want to be alone for much longer. Elevators dinged and stairwells started to echo with people.

From the fridge, I grabbed a few lattes and put them into to-go bags. After a quick perusal, I decided on their soup and sandwich combo, thoroughly reading the ingredient list. No shellfish. I read it again. *No shellfish.* I put everything into her bag and made my way to the east wing elevator.

It creaked up to our floor, and when I stepped out into the hall, I was relieved to see that her door was still closed and all was quiet inside. I crept in, noticing her writing at the desk. She was focused, intense, and I didn't want to interrupt that, but she needed to eat.

"Delivery," I said softly, careful not to startle her. Her face brightened when she looked back. She closed her eyes and inhaled deeply, letting a smile cross her face.

"That smells delicious!" Relief flooded me.

"Made sure it was allergen free for you, and I

grabbed these." When I produced the latte bottles, it was almost like she'd forgotten about the food. "It might be a long night."

She took everything and set it out on her desk. I put her laptop and files beside her.

"Thank you, Heath. I appreciate everything you've done today. I mean that."

I waved a hand to dismiss the gratitude as I sat beside her on the bed. "It was nothing, I promise. What can I help you with? We can go back to the records room tomorrow, hopefully with no trouble from unwanted guests." Her brow furrowed and her head tilted as she leaned in close.

Soft inhales filled the space as she continued to move around me. "You smell really good and almost . . ."

"Almost what?"

"It'd be impossible," she whispered, shaking her head. "Sweet and smokey maybe?" Blair moved closer to my chest and up my neck.

"You didn't have this reaction earlier—"

"Tobacco?" I knew every note she smelled and could tell her all of them, but I liked her odd closeness. This was unlike the Blair front she'd put on so far for everyone.

"Bad habits can be hard to quit." I gripped her bedspread tighter when she moved and the tip of her nose brushed my neck.

"There's an herbal scent, too."

"Rosemary," I answered, on the precipice of asking if she was part bloodhound. Her hand was featherlight on my shoulder as she steadied herself.

"Liquor?" I nodded in response, unsure if she could even register the movement.

"Bourbon, if you're looking for specifics." Hair fell over her shoulder and I brushed it back, careful not to touch her.

"But what's sweet?"

"Caramel, vanilla . . ." *You.*

"I'm sorry, that was odd, but it did confirm my thoughts." She moved back, abandoning the questioning and sniffing. She didn't look relieved or satisfied. Instead, it felt like even more wheels were turning.

"Stranger things have happened in Aspendale Manor, Blair." *My little weirdo.*

Her face was red, a shade so dark and deep, I'd never seen on someone before. Pointedly, she looked everywhere else but at me. With her laptop open, she explained her task again.

"I, uh, have to correct the patient's diagnosis and find the medical errors." Without another word, she ate her lunch and read the case study. I watched her trade off between taking bites and notes. I could've used the excuse of committing her to memory, but she had a spot there easy enough without even trying.

"Do you want me to leave?" She looked at me with wide eyes.

"No, not at all," she rushed out. She didn't want me to leave, but there was also nothing for me to help with. I didn't want our partnership getting off on a false start. I'd do the damn case study for her if she asked.

"Mind if I nap?"

"Knock yourself out." She snickered to herself. I lay back on her bed, the sheets and pillows sending her scent all around me. She smelled pretty, like lilacs and something else. Something...

Loud chimes rang out in my subconscious, and I sat up, startled. I counted eight and couldn't believe I'd slept in her bed for so damn long. I blinked away the tiredness, and my eyes settled on a bag at the foot of her bed. A sticky note sat on top of it.

Heath, thank you again.

Eat, stay.
B

Blair had brought me dinner. I'd slept the day away and yet she'd gone back to get me . . .

The sound of a shower caught my attention. Without knocking the food over, I stood and made my way across the room quietly. As I stood in the doorway of her bathroom, words were lost on me. The sunset illuminated her silhouette behind the curtain and the faintest voice humming hit my ears. Blair seemed happy and content, finally. My intrusion would've tipped that on its side.

She'd asked me to stay, but she deserved her alone time after today. I walked back, grabbing the food and looking over her case study. She'd made copies and marked the file to hell with highlighter and pen, and a full document sat on her laptop perfectly replicated with her changes. She'd finished her task. Pride swelled inside me.

I opened her door quietly and slipped out.

"Goodnight, Blair," I whispered to myself before going to my suite. Her sticky note was everything in that moment, and I stuck it to a page in the notebook for her.

Eating was lonelier than I'd anticipated. It felt like the rest of the night would go like that as I stepped into the shower, wondering if leaving had been the right decision. The water was hot against my skin, but it did wonders releasing the tension in my shoulders.

I thought over the day, going back and forth on my choice to leave. I'd wanted to stay, and I hoped she knew that at the very least. My thoughts wandered from there.

Wandered to Blair herself.

Blair's deliciously dark hair that was a direct contrast to mine. Dark eyes. The column of her throat. Her hands, long fingers, and nails that could shred skin easily. She was in front of me, striking and mysterious. Not physically, but Blair all the same.

Turning the water cold for a few seconds, I cleared my mind before stepping out and drying off. I wrapped the towel around my hips and made my way to the dresser. Rummaging through clothes, I tried to prepare for tomorrow mentally. It'd be taxing, especially with the not-so-friendly apparition following us around. Paired with a daily daunting task, this would compound over time. But that was the point, no? Aspendale wanted to weed out anyone unfit to work under pressure. Albeit, supernatural pressure hadn't been on my list.

I pulled out a pair of sweatpants just as a loud crash echoed through our corridor. A scream came before the footsteps. It almost sounded like my name.

Blair.

Before I could make it across the room, she ran inside, slamming my door behind her and barreling right into me.

"Blair?" I wrapped my arms around her shoulders, suddenly all too aware that I was still naked. She pulled away from me and pointed toward her room while crying nonsense.

"There's—it's—" She was petrified and violently shaking where she stood. Tears streamed down her face, and I did my best to wipe them away.

"Shh, it's okay." I pulled her back into my arms, and when her door slammed over and over, I got a clue as to what she could've been dealing with moments prior.

"I'm going crazy."

"No, you're not." The thought about pants

entered my head again. "Give me a minute, okay?" I ran off to change, and when I came back, she was curled up on my bed, and the sight broke my heart.

"It felt like something touched me. It hurt, and I freaked out because nothing was there, but I felt it, right? That's crazy. I'm going mad," she said as I sat down beside her.

"I can take a look." I trailed my hand down her back. She wasn't in the best pajamas for this, but I offered anyway. She hissed when I moved over her side. "Let me see."

She pulled up the big T-shirt and revealed three large, deep scratches. They started at her hip, just above her underwear, and traveled up, over her ribs and onto her back.

"What is it?" But she knew, she had to know by now.

"I need that beautiful mind to be very open right now. I've asked you before, but are you ready to believe in spirits, Blair?"

"They're not—" she started, raising her voice, but I was done with the skepticism at this point.

She could turn her nose up at apparitions and noises, but these scratches weren't something she could brush off so easily. I flipped her over on the bed and pinned her down, grabbing my phone and taking a picture. I practically shoved the photo in her face and she gasped.

Realizing the compromising position I'd put us in, I backed off her and let her have the phone.

"I'll delete that, by the way," I assured her. "But Blair, I need one thing from you. Can I see your hands?" She dropped my phone and held them out. Taking them in mine, I turned them over and looked at her nails. There was no trace of blood, but though I felt like a right ass for doing so, I needed to check and be sure.

"This can't be possible," she said, nearly crying again.

"Something has latched onto you. It doesn't seem to be confined to the records room, and this feels more violent. Want to get rid of it? I need you to trust me."

"I trust you," she whispered weakly. She looked defeated, and I sighed, cupping her face and guiding her to watch my eyes as I promised I'd keep her safe.

A bloodcurdling scream came from the floor below as I started to speak and tears filled her eyes.

"Not our problem, right? Sleep," I demanded. I brought her toward the side of the mattress against the wall and pulled the comforter up to her shoulders, and she tucked herself into my chest as more screams filled the air. They were awful, and I pressed her into me, covering one ear with my hand.

"Don't listen."

FIVE
THE MISSING AND THE LOST

HEATH

LEANING ON THE DESK, I watched through the open window. It was overcast again, and there was a storm rolling in. The unlit cigarette in my hand called to me. I'd told myself quitting for the Aspendale internship would be ideal, and I'd managed for the most part. But lately . . .

Soft, quiet footsteps entered my room, and I'd know them anywhere in any crowd. Somehow hesitant *and* sure. Certain of herself, yet uncertain that she belonged. *What a conundrum, this one.*

The scent of her freshly washed hair hit me next.

"Ms. Blair," I said before she had the chance to

officially announce herself. "How lovely it is to see you." My back was still to her, but it was a sure bet that she'd be lovely. Her steps moved closer, and I continued to watch the dark clouds rapidly moving in. The desk beneath me jostled as she sat herself atop it. That caught my attention, and I looked over my shoulder at her.

Her hair was down in large waves that framed her angular face beautifully. Her hand moved across my desk, and it was only when she flicked my lighter open that I realized her intention. I placed the cigarette between my lips, leaning forward in the flame to light it from her hand. I exhaled, holding it out as I looked at it and questioned when I really would quit.

Her hand grabbed my wrist as she moved the cigarette closer. She wrapped her crimson lips around it and inhaled, letting the smoke swirl with enticement. The lipstick-stained filter sat there, provoking me to taste her. Begging me to feel her lips pressed to mine.

I let the thoughts dissipate on another drag, watching her in silence. She took the cigarette from me, and we shared quiet exchanges until we reached the near end. She looked at me with a curious grin.

"Was I not supposed to let you smoke?" She

couldn't have known, but no, she shouldn't have let me indulge in her temptations. "Teasing aside, we're late. We've done a lot, but I'm not sure how we are in comparison. Also, I wanted to say thank you again and that I appreciate—"

"Why are you here, Blair?" My words weren't harsh. They were soft, pained, even full of longing. "Not that I don't enjoy your company. I've just been under the impression that you don't casually enjoy mine."

"I enjoy you just fine," she says, clipped in tone and offended, but her word choice caught up to her. Blair's cheeks burned red, brighter even when the lightning flash caught them. "Your casual company."

"My casual company," I repeated. Little Blair wanted to jump from topic to topic. I'd oblige her. Anything she needed, she'd have.

"I also wanted to ask you about supernatural things. My concerns, your help. I'd like you to teach me about this."

I took another drag of the cigarette, and the overlap of our lips on the filter drove me mad. "Have a seat."

"I'm sitting." *Her defiance* . . .

"In the chair, please, Ms. Blair."

"Ms. Blair this, Ms. Blair *that*," she mocked me.

"Mr.. . ." She wanted to continue, but her quizzical brow told me she was searching for information she didn't know. She would've said Heath if she wasn't looking for . . .

"You don't remember my last name. You didn't look at the email?" She hopped off the desk with a huff and crossed her arms over her chest.

"I looked at the important parts," she grumbled with rosy cheeks. Moving closer, I inhaled and the cigarette burned, but the red tip paled in comparison to Blair's embarrassed cheeks.

"Crowley," I whispered, letting the smoke hang in the small distance between us.

"Mr. Crowley," she teased. "I need something."

I waited, letting her have the time and space to collect her thoughts as she stepped back and put distance between us.

"I need an explanation of sorts. In the annex, I could understand, but when I opened my room on the first day, there was this distinct scent, and I have to know." She stopped there, not daring to accuse or explain further.

"No," I said, assuming her intent. "I wasn't there for any weird reason. I promise."

"Then how—"

"Sit in the chair, Ms. Blair," I interrupted,

pointing to the office chair to her right. Her arms crossed over her chest; she didn't seem to like being told what to do. "No matter," I whispered to myself before grabbing her by the hips and putting her in the seat.

I sat on the desk in front of her. She wanted a teacher, she'd get one.

"Simply, I walked into the wrong room that morning." I put out my cigarette, lighting another one thanks to her persuasion from earlier. She sat in silence as I picked through various books on my table and stacked them beside me. "Well, I say the wrong room. I asked Cressida if I could have the other one. The view was better."

"I guess that's better than you being a stalker."

"Harsh words." She eyed the stack of books.

"Harsh manor." I nodded in silent agreement. This place was rough and growing harder to deal with on a day-to-day basis. "This place is weird, right? It's not me?"

The frown on her brow cut deep as she looked up to me for reassurance. Her brown eyes were large and glistening with tears threatening to form. I reached out and tucked a piece of hair behind her ear.

Before I could offer the reassurance she sought,

her face lit up from the flash of lightning, and loud thunder cracked. The room shook as it rolled through the sky and she jumped, looking out the window to now darkened clouds.

"Scared of a little storm, Blair?"

"I'm not scared of anything, Heath." The way she said my name . . . "This place is weird; I can accept weird, and I can find the answer to it."

She stood, barely coming face-to-face with me as her eyes looked me up and down. Blair took the books from the table.

"Read those," I said as she turned and headed for the door.

"I gathered that," she quipped, watching as I took another drag and let the smoke linger in the growing distance between us. "We need to get to our tasks for the day; we're a few hours late."

"Not my fault," I teased before she could step through the frame. She looked back, her eyebrows pinched and her mind likely turning with the ways she wanted to murder me. My mouth tipped into a grin, and she rolled those big brown eyes.

"When you say it like that, it sounds scandalous."

"You wanted to sleep with me," I taunted, pushing all the luck and buttons I could. I didn't want her to leave yet. The back and forth kept her here seconds longer. It didn't matter that I'd be following after her soon enough. I wanted her with me out of public view.

"Stop saying it like that! I wanted to sleep *in*. There's a major difference, Mr. Crowley." She bit my name out with embarrassed anger that made me want to wrap her up in my arms and take her back to bed with me. Innocently, of course. That was the best sleep I'd had since . . .

"Are you flirting with me?" Another crack of thunder made her jump and signaled the extent of my luck. I raised my brow, daring her to say yes.

"In your nightmares."

I let her go then, satisfied and content with my morning. The smile on my face was permanent as she disappeared down the hall. I took out my notebook for her and immediately sketched her scowl.

What a beautiful, angry, little Blair.

SHE WAS at the task board when I managed to make my way downstairs. The energy in the room was off. Not supernatural, but anxious. People were in hushed conversations and frantically looking around as though they were watching their backs. I passed by Cressida's office and the door was cracked, her voice filtering through.

"I don't know . . . was terrible . . . I won't say anything . . . know by morning." I only caught fragments from her, but none of it sounded like the news to come would be good.

Looking at Blair, I noticed her hands were atop her hips as she stared at the board. She wore a burgundy turtleneck and a fitted black pencil skirt. Her legs were defined by her black stilettos. Something I'd noticed was that she was always dressed for the job. People had leaned heavily on the casual side of business casual, except Blair. She always looked exceptional.

The only time I'd seen her completely dressed down was last night.

I walked up beside her, expecting a reaction but getting nothing in return.

"Blair?"

"Do you see it?" she asked, never looking away from the task board. Four envelopes were left.

"See what?"

"The names, Heath." She was exasperated, chewing at her bottom lip as her brow furrowed. I reached out with my thumb and freed her lip from her teeth.

"The names, ours are up there." She glanced at me before reaching up and taking out our envelopes. Two remained.

"Thom and Clarice."

"I can read. That was kind of a requirement." Her scowl returned, served right to me, just as I wanted.

"You can read but can you comprehend? Make connections?"

"Blair—"

"The screams last night. The horrific night we just experienced. Clarice isn't here. She was bubbly, in everyone's group, and no one's seen her." My mind drifted back to the interns and their hushed conversations. Then to Cressida's, but I wouldn't worry Blair over that right now.

"You think Clarice is missing?"

"And I don't think Thom made it a full day."

"Are we going on a paranormal investigation into the hells of Aspendale Manor?" I teased, but she didn't smile. Not a muscle moved in her stern face.

"I think something weird has happened. And I think there's an answer we can find. Will you join me?" she asked, handing me the envelope marked with my name in Cressida's penmanship.

"Always, dear Blair."

SIX
NOTHING IS AS IT APPEARS

BLAIR

SINCE HEATH HAD VISITED my room with promises to make it better, it'd been easier and more comfortable to be in here. He hadn't told me everything he'd done, but I also didn't want to know. Reading through the texts, I'd gathered an idea, but I wasn't ready for his conclusions.

The weekend approached and with it, I hoped for rest and relaxation. Dr. Aspendale had had tough demands for the first week, but my stack of completed projects grew with each day and my Saturday submission would be a weight off my shoulders. Unexpectedly, Heath did manage to help as he promised. We pushed each other forward and collaborated surprisingly well. He was . . . interesting. I couldn't quite pin my feelings down yet, but I enjoyed his help and growing friendship.

Some people walked around like zombies, the lack of sleep evident. They were close to crumbling under the pressure.

I smoothed down my blouse and stepped into the hallway, making my way to the annex. Heath's door was closed, and while it wasn't unusual, he was known to wait for me in the mornings. I didn't let myself expand on what that meant for him.

The click of my heels across the floor was dampened by the carpeted area near the board. Envelopes remained today, but mine wasn't one of them. Something I hadn't expected was the compiled envelopes. No one had cleared Thom's basket from the start, and more came as the days passed. Clarice now had two in her basket.

Mine and Heath's were empty.

I pulled out my phone.

Blair: Did you grab my envelope?

Heath: No, I'm upstairs.

Weird.

I pocketed my phone. It was likely Aspendale didn't have a task for me . . . or us. Friday could've been Aspendale's idea of a catch-up day. Considering my week was complete, I left the annex and explored the main house. Up the winding grand staircase, I passed the floor with the lovely and ever-exciting records room. I kept ascending. I'd been to the second floor once this week, but I hadn't been able to familiarize myself with it.

Down its hall, various rooms and labels occupied the area. One in particular caught my attention at the end. It was the only wooden door with a window. The glass was distorted and frosted, making it hard to see inside. A dusty plaque was screwed into the wall, and I wiped it down.

"Laboratory," I whispered to myself. Counting on it being locked, I tried the knob anyway. It gave effortlessly and the door hinges groaned open.

Inside were steel slabs and tables like in a morgue. I looked around; there was even a body cooler. The square doors unsettled me, so I turned to the real laboratory part. There were aisles of shelves. This place was deceptively large from the inside. The pharmacology instruments had me wishing for tasks related to this specialty. It was colder than the hallway, and while the plaque had had dust, the instruments did not.

I walked the aisles and looked over the shelves, picking up jars and beakers as I read the labels.

The door opened, and I turned around to see a smiling Heath. His grin was irritating, but unfortunately his full smile was a sight to behold.

"There you are," he said gently as he strolled toward me. "I was looking all over the place for you." Standing in front of me, he slid his hands into his pockets.

"Sorry, I didn't have an envelope so I thought I'd look around. I didn't think to text you and ask if you wanted to join."

I set the vial I was holding back in its place and smoothed my hands over my blouse. Since the other night, in simple moments I found myself nervous around Heath. He wasn't unpredictable, quite the opposite. And I didn't know how to handle the slow shift we were experiencing.

He'd been right the other day. I had wanted to sleep in, but I'd also enjoyed that I had slept in with him.

I closed the distance between us, and he sat atop one of the tables. When I was within reach, he took my hand and ran it over his chest and down his thigh. My cheeks burned red.

"Heath—"

"We've been doing this little dance..." His hand trapped mine. His grip grew tighter.

"Have we?" I asked, a little uncertain and confused by the way his mood excited me. With speed, he pulled me into him. My hips hit the metal table between his legs and I hissed, just before a yawn escaped me.

"Tired already?" I blinked slowly through his question.

"Late nights are catching up to me, I guess." His fingers stroked my cheeks, so featherlight that I almost didn't feel it. Except for the chill in their wake.

"Can I ask you something, Blair Grimm?" He tipped my face up to his and my eyes fluttered closed.

"My full name, must be something serious." I yawned again. I was so tired.

"How do you feel about me?"

"How do I feel about Heath Crowley?" I repeated back to him. "Well . . . that's hard to answer. How much should we know about someone before we can say we know feelings are there? I know little pieces of you." I blinked my eyes open, fighting the exhaustion. "I like what I've come to know, but I think there's more you could show me."

I grinned as my phone buzzed in my pocket. Holding up a finger, I looked down to read the incoming text. Frozen in terror and shock, I read the message twice.

> Heath: Hey, where did you run off to?

I looked up at "Heath" and watched those silvery blue eyes turn into a mass of black. His beautiful face fell into that of a frightening, disfigured shadow. I jumped back, regaining clarity with each step I took. My shoulder hit one of the shelves and pain shot down my arm. I staggered to the door, but I didn't look away from that nightmare that mocked me.

"What's the matter with little Blair Grimm?" The voice wasn't Heath's, overlayed and deep—it was sinister. Demonic.

"Don't come near me!" I screamed, bolting for the door and running through the hall. I cried out as I approached the staircase. "Heath! Heath!" I continued screaming as I ran down toward the first floor. I chanced a look back but saw nothing. "Heath!"

My heart raced, and I feared it'd stop altogether from fright.

"Blair?" I collided with Heath on the stairs, and

he steadied me, pulling me close and looking me over. "Why are you screaming?"

I watched his eyes. Silvery blue as always, no trace of darkness to be found. His features weren't sinister and twisted, his voice normal. Without thinking, I grabbed his face and pulled him down.

His lips met mine, stunned and uncertain. But I kissed him again. And again. I pulled him into me, sliding my tongue along his lip until he slipped his into my mouth. He groaned. This was Heath. His hands wove into my hair, and he pressed against the back of my head, not letting me pull away.

"Making sure you're real," I whispered against his lips. He moved my head for better access as he explored.

"Doing this with everyone?"

"Just you." His tongue stroked mine and he pulled my bottom lip between his teeth.

"Only me." He brought me to him, making me stand on my toes even in heels. He devoured me like a mad man, and I didn't want to stop him. I couldn't bring myself to do so.

His hands released me like my skin had burned him. "No, I-I . . . Gods, yes." He was on me again in an instant, soft, slow kisses as he whined into my open mouth. "Yes, yes," he said, licking over my tongue before pulling back. "But no, fuck. This . . . Don't look at me like that."

"Like what?"

"Like you want to fuck me." His hand covered my eyes, and I felt his deep breaths move his chest. "Fuck, I just might let you," he murmured, kissing me again. He groaned as he forced himself to stop. "No, no. Something happened," he said, moving back at arm's length as he stepped down and turned away, adjusting his pants. "Don't leave that spot, tell me what happened."

"I can't leave this spot?" He turned around, shock marring his face.

"I will fuck you against that wall if you kiss me again. What happened, Blair?" Heath ran his hands through his white-blond hair, breathing heavily while eyeing me.

"In the lab, you were in the lab, but then it wasn't you because you texted me, a-and then that thing just became a monster." I took a deep, shaky breath, and he grabbed my hands. His touch was solid and warm. I looked down at his firm grasp.

"And the . . . the, um . . ."

"It touched me," I whispered. "I almost couldn't feel it. It was ice cold, and I figured—"

"I wouldn't be?" He laughed. He dropped one of

his hands and pulled me down the stairs. "Okay, okay. It's fine. Let's, uh, get away from whatever the fuck that was, alright?" He moved us with haste, and I almost had to run.

When we arrived in the annex, Cressida stopped us.

"To your quarters, everyone." Her face showed no emotion, stoic as ever.

"What, why?" I asked, ignoring that Heath was still holding my hand.

"There's been an accident," she said coldly and completely unaffected.

"An accident?" Cressida looked fed up with our inquisition, but Heath was ready to press again.

"It's an intern. That's all I can tell you at the moment." Cressida walked away, and Heath pulled me into his hold. I looked at the task board, my mind reeling over all the pieces.

"Heath," I whispered, and he hummed in response. "What if it wasn't an accident?"

"Upstairs," he demanded, racing us up the east wing stairwell and to his suite.

HEATH

She sat on my bed, and I continued to stare out

the window. I hadn't looked at her since we'd come to the suite. I couldn't. That kiss . . . that misplaced, earth-shattering kiss.

That woman.

"Do you think the missing intern was Clarice and they found her?" I asked, more so to distract myself from my thoughts. An eidetic memory was a pain in the ass in these moments. While she pondered the question, I took steadying breaths. I rubbed my finger over my thumb, begging myself to give in and have a smoke.

"Yes, but I also think you're right about the spirits," she whispered sheepishly, clearing her throat. "I don't think it was an accident, and I think whatever is haunting the main house is what hurt her," she said more assuredly.

I recalled the scratches down Blair's back. What I'd heard and witnessed myself, it had been violent. It had seemed to grow bolder by the day.

"And you want to . . ." I turned around then, wishing I hadn't but so grateful I did.

"Get rid of the ghosts?" She sounded confused, and her statement caught me so off guard I found myself chuckling. "I don't know the words! This is my first official day!"

"Getting rid of them is perfectly fine, but you

need to learn," I said, walking around the corner and sitting on my desk.

"Are you going to quiz me, *professor?*" Her tone was laced with sarcasm, but all the same my heart stopped. I stopped moving, thinking, breathing.

"Absolutely," I said, snapping back into it. "If you can't remember the difference between a ghost and a demon, then you're fucked."

She smirked, and I reached over, giving her one of the other books I'd kept for myself. Out of the corner of my eye, movement in the circle caught my attention.

"Blair," I whispered like a fool; no one could hear me from the grounds. I watched closely as white vans and a cop pulled through the drive and parked. "Come here."

"What?" She tried to look out the window, but she was too short to see what I needed her to. I made space on my desk and helped her stand on it. She leaned into the window, peering down at the grounds.

"The drive, what do you see?"

"Um, a cop and some white vans?" She shifted, trying to look closer.

"What don't you see?" I moved to the window beside her. Her eyes scanned over everything.

"An ambulance," she said proudly. I steadied my hand on her hip.

"Yes, and?" Her brow scrunched at my question.

"There's no logo."

Blair's breath hitched, and I saw what had caught her attention. A gurney was wheeled out from the annex and into one of the white vans. A crow flew to the branches and watched us as we spied. An unexpected squawk from the little creature made Blair shriek and duck down.

I fell into laughter as she looked up at me, whispering, "Is this our first investigation?" Her excitement delighted me.

"If you want it to be."

She slid off my desk and smoothed her hands over her blouse and skirt. "Can I ask you a question and it not sound silly?"

"You can ask me anything, Blair."

"Could I—or, could you . . . um."

She paused and her eyes dropped to my mouth. Without a word, I reached out and grabbed her throat in a gentle, firm grasp. I traced my thumb along her jaw, stopping under her chin and tilting her head back.

I kissed her once, twice, three times, the lightest and softest touches.

"I also want to know more about you," she whispered against my lips. I kissed her again; she was addictive.

"That can be arranged," I said, sliding my hand up her side as she traced hers up and over my chest. She moved across my shoulders and down my arms. Blair brought me in for a kiss.

"I'm thirty-two," I whispered between her pecks. "I'm an October Scorpio." Her tongue traced my bottom lip. "This is my natural blond."

She laughed, and I peppered her cheeks with my kisses. My arms found their way around her waist and I hoisted her up.

"I have an eidetic memory, I prefer cats over dogs, and I'm addicted to you, Blair Grimm."

She laughed at that and asked, "Addicted to me?" I picked her up and walked toward my bed, innocent in nature, but it made her cheeks flush.

"Since you accepted my arm and walked to dinner with me." I grazed my nose over her cheek and set her on the mattress. "Actually, it was the way you looked at me with so much indifference when you first got here."

She gasped. "I did not!"

I laughed but said nothing more to the contrary as I pushed her shoulders back and rolled her over. I slipped her heels off and dropped them on my floor. I trailed a hand up her exposed calf, kissing my way up just below the apex of her thighs before going down the other side.

"It worsened when you ran into my bed, needing me . . . wanting me." I bit her calf gently, but enough to leave an impression of my teeth. "I'll never recover from today."

I crawled over her, nuzzling into her neck and taking in the scent of her perfume. Lilacs and coconut, from her conditioner. It was my favorite. Scooping her into a hug, I rolled onto my back and held her to my side as giggles escaped her.

"Later, I promise," I whispered into her hair. I reached behind me and grabbed the book from my bedside table. I handed it to her. "Read."

SEVEN
SECRETS IN THE LIBRARY

BLAIR

I WALKED UP to Heath's door hesitantly with the closed door. He always expected my entrance, so I tried the doorknob. It stopped short of a full turn. His door had never been locked before either.

"Heath," I called, knocking twice and waiting. Grumbles came from the other side, and after the lock disengaged, a grumpy Heath opened the door.

"Yeah," he huffed, his face pinched and eyes hardly open. "Oh, Blair, hi," he said. His expression softened and a lazy smile replaced the scowl.

"I wanted to see if you were up for the library today."

"Yeah, come in, come in." Heath stepped back and opened the door fully. He wore only sweatpants, and I loved the dressed down and disheveled look. His white hair was mussed and tossed as though he had just rolled out of bed when I knocked. He raised his arms as he stretched and walked off toward his bathroom. I looked around for the best place to sit, but the bed and desk were in equal disarray.

I chose the bed.

His mattress was soft but firm like mine, only his sheets smelled like him. I listened as the water ran briefly and he rummaged through a drawer. He appeared suddenly with dripping hair that he toweled dry and a half-hearted attempt at getting dressed. His shirt was only unbuttoned and exposed a nice portion of his chest. It was half tucked into his slacks. He tossed the towel and grabbed a cardigan from the back of his desk chair. Heath walked to the door and looked back at me as I sat unmoving.

"You comin'?" I hadn't even told him why I wanted to go to the library. In my stunned silence, he doubled back across the room and stood over me. He shook his head like a dog, flinging the last droplets of his wet hair onto me.

"What the hell?" I said, standing.

"She moves and speaks! Impressive, Ms. Blair." I glared at him, but he only winked in return.

"What's wrong with you?" I shrieked, wiping water from my face.

"You'll learn in due time. Shall we?" He nodded, and I led the way with frustrated stomps.

In the annex, we decided on a quick breakfast we could carry with us as we made our way to the library. He chose yogurt and I grabbed a burrito.

"So, why were you cranky this morning?"

"What do you mean?" he asked, scooping his spoon around the side of the container.

"Your door was closed and when you answered it, you were cranky and huffy."

"I wouldn't say huffy," he mumbled. "I didn't get a lot of sleep last night. I finished off the last pieces of my tasks and got maybe three hours?" He looked at me apologetically. "Didn't mean to be short with you initially. I didn't know who was at my door. Typically, you just walk in."

"Door was locked."

"Keeping the ghosts out," he retorted, smiling around his bite of yogurt.

THE LIBRARY WAS grand and old, a perfect Victorian era dream. Modern books were mixed with old, clothbound copies. I wondered how many first editions and rare pieces the Aspendale family had to their name.

Heath wandered over to a table, his brow puzzled as his hand traced over the texts.

"Do you ever feel like some things are just too easy?" he asked as he picked up a book.

"Sure, but I also believe that sometimes there's a simple answer for it that you're overlooking. Why?" I walked up beside him and looked over the titles on the table.

"Conveniently enough, the books I wanted to look at are already pulled and just lying here?" I shrugged my shoulders at his paranoia.

"Other interns could be in haunted rooms; you never know." He looked down at me, but he didn't continue.

I wasn't sure what we were looking for, but I made all kinds of notes as we spent the next few hours flipping through those books. I noticed Heath didn't make any, and I wondered if he really did have an eidetic memory.

"I can't do this," he said, exasperated and more annoyed than this morning.

"What's wrong?"

"It's so cliché, you know? There are decades of rumors floating around about the manor and how it's a paranormal beacon, but isn't it a little odd that there are several records mixed in with these books that point straight to a portal?" His hands were on his hips, and he looked at each title again.

"Do you want the logical answer?"

"I know the—" He paused. "Enlighten me, dear Blair. You make it all better."

His temper was flaring, but I knew it wasn't toward me. He wanted answers, not to be played with.

"Someone is setting it up. It's too perfect. Everything is laid out for every answer. That's not how it should be. Information should take time."

"You're a brilliant woman, you know?" He sighed and let his shoulders relax. "Let's go to the estate's records."

He took my hand in his and led me through the ancient library. Aspendale likely had no reason to come in here, and with hardly anyone occupying the main house these days, the library was left to collect dust.

He pulled a few journals and loose papers while I stood there uselessly.

"Can I kiss you, Blair?" he asked, his back to me as he looked for more things on the shelf. I was grateful for that; my face wore the shock and embarrassment that turned my stomach.

"Why?"

HEATH

Of all the things for her to have asked, *why* wasn't what I expected. She damn well knew why; she'd started it in the stairwell. I'd never recover from that kiss. I'd told her as much.

"Because I want to," I said, turning around and keeping the shock off my face that she'd ask such a thing. "Your lips are perfectly red and completely unkissed today. Can I kiss you?" I stepped closer. Her chest brushed mine with each breath she took as I waited.

"Yes," she said, so quiet I almost missed it. I grabbed her like a mad man, like a starved man. Because I was.

Mad and starved.

Starved and mad.

This damned woman had me craving that which

drove me insane after just one taste. No better did the third or fourth bite satisfy me, as she was an incurable hunger. So, I took. And I took.

I pushed Blair against the back wall and dropped my hands under her thighs. She was light in my arms as I hoisted her up. With each pass of my grinding hips, she bucked and writhed against me.

Fuck, fuck, fuck.

"I want to fuck you, Blair," I said, and she gasped. "So, so disrespectfully, too." I gave no room for an answer as I took her mouth with mine again. Her response was her hands finding my pants and unfastening the button. "I don't have condoms. Is that okay?"

I wanted her, needed her like air. I needed to be inside her, to feel her around me. The noises she made, so soft and submissive. Willing and begging.

"Yes, please . . ."

I traced my nose along her jaw, ready to kiss down her pretty neck when a shadow caught my attention. My thoughts lapsed for a moment, and she pulled me to her, refusing to let me stop. I kissed down her throat, peppering small bites along her flesh as I traveled down to her chest. Soft, smooth, and devoid of bruises.

No, no. That won't do.

I bit and sucked until purplish bruises appeared in the wake of my lips. Her legs squeezed me tighter with each one. Blair's fingers wove through my hair and trapped me to her skin. I couldn't leave even if I wanted to. The way she moaned through the painful kisses made my cock ache. Louder and louder. I didn't care if Aspendale himself heard her.

I slid my hand to her soaked pussy, teasing her with soft strokes over her clit. Ever so gently did I press inside, just an inch or so. She was tight and slick for me.

"Heath," she said over the sound of a thump on the ground. I paused my musings and her cries died down so that I could listen. The creaks and groans of wood caught my attention now. The same noise came again as books fell. "Heath!"

I moved out of the aisle with Blair held close to my chest as I covered her head. A book stack fell against the wall with a loud crash as books and journals spilled onto the floor. I pressed my forehead to Blair's; our panted breaths mingled and our noses brushed as we recuperated.

"You okay?" I asked after the literal dust settled around us. She nodded, and I slid her off me, fixing her clothes before adjusting mine. I kissed her again.

"I don't think we did that, baby," I whispered across her lips.

"Do you think someone else is in here?"

"I think . . ." I waited, choosing the right words for this moment. "I saw a shadow. Human or otherwise, I'm not sure. It caught my attention just before the books fell. It could go either way," I said, leaving it open for her.

"It'd make more sense that someone else was in here, but why do that? It could've killed us."

"If someone's killing interns, that'd be their goal then. But the motivation is still lost on me. Why go through so much effort to make it look like some sort of haunting?"

"I thought you said—"

"No, no, your experiences are very real and true. I've witnessed it myself. There are two things happening at once. Someone is abusing the legends and lore of the manor to get away with heinous crimes, and you, my dear, are being haunted by something."

"What do we do?" she asked, her brown eyes wide and round. I hadn't concluded that far yet.

"We should tell . . . Cressida?"

"Why is that a question?" She huffed, crossing her arms.

"Because I don't trust anyone that I wasn't about to fuck three minutes ago. If my hands weren't on their body, I don't trust their whereabouts." I grabbed her hand and led her back through the library.

"So, we go to Cressida, then."

"We go to Cressida," I repeated.

I had the worst feeling twist in my gut. I didn't like the prospect of that one bit.

EIGHT
THE SECRETARY

HEATH

WE WAITED a day to collect ourselves and our findings. It was too obvious, too easy to find information that would've sent others on their merry way. Ignorance was bliss, or so they said. Death seemed to accompany bliss in Aspendale Manor.

"Are you ready?" Blair asked as she waltzed into my suite.

I turned around, slamming my notebook closed where I'd been drawing her. I'd fixated on her chest from last night, flushed and heavy while we'd nearly fucked in the library. The way her blouse had bunched and draped over her body was a beautiful study.

"I'm ready," I rushed out, quick to stand and put distance between the notebook and myself.

"What were you up to?" she asked, trying to peek around me. I grabbed her face, kissing her and derailing her want to snoop.

"Thinking about you, missing you." She eyed me, squinting and evaluating my words. Half-truths, whole truths. It wasn't something I wanted her to know about yet and I hoped she'd drop the topic.

"Oddly sweet, but there's no time. We have to go." She took my hand, and I fell in step with her.

Downstairs, it was a ghost town. We'd been told to take the day off—the day we'd already had off—and to mourn. Blair had been right: Clarice had gone missing and had been found in her quarters. There had been an "accident." No information had been given other than that, and it struck me as odd. Without any concrete evidence to the contrary, this would prove difficult.

Cressida's office was down by the dining hall. The door was closed when we approached. I knocked first. No response.

"Do you think she's out?" Blair whispered.

"Where does she go? What does she do?"

"I don't think I can recall seeing her anywhere outside of the annex if I'm being honest." Blair opened her mouth to say something, but a light voice startled both of us.

"Mr. Crowley, Ms. Grimm." Cressida stood behind us. "What can I help you with today? Your tasks were completed on time, and today is a day of rest, need I remind you."

"Yes, ma'am, we're aware," Blair said first, and Cressida's nose crinkled for just a second at the mention of *ma'am*. "We want to talk to you about some concerns we have."

"By all means, come in." Cressida stepped between us and unlocked the door. Her keyring was massive and had dozens of keys. I looked at Blair behind Cressida's back and nodded toward her. Understanding shone in her eyes. Cressida could go anywhere and do anything she pleased.

Her office was sterile and bland. There wasn't a single piece of personalization or affection.

"We think there's some foul play going on," I said, noting that Cressida's eyes narrowed despite a smile starting.

"Whatever do you mean, Mr. Crowley?"

"You said what happened to Clarice was an accident, but what we heard—"

"You heard nothing," she said firmly, cutting me off before I could finish.

"We heard Clarice—"

"You heard nothing," she repeated, opening a planner and looking through a few pages. "Clarice was in the west wing. You two—" she eyed us—"are in the east wing. Are you not?"

"We are, but—"

"Then you were not physically able to discern what happened. I know you're aware of the manor's reputation. Don't fall prey to ghost tales, Mr. Crowley." She shut the book and leaned back in her chair.

"That's what I'm trying to say—"

"Mr. Crowley." My name was snapped from her lips, and I sat straighter from the ice it was laced with.

"Yes, ma'am. We're sorry to have bothered you." I stood up, taking Blair's hand and not missing how it caught Cressida's attention.

I TAPPED my pen hard on my desk. Cressida had been a disappointment regarding this, but there was more to it. Her demeanor hadn't just been dismissive. It had been indifferent. She'd shown more interest in us than anything.

"Heath?"

"Hmm? I'm sorry, I was distracted." The frown she wore told me I'd been checked out for a while.

"I was asking if you wanted to go to Dr. Aspendale. We tried Cressida, but maybe he'd understand and not be so dismissive over an intern's death." Her eyes looked between mine, and I tapped my pen again, thinking it over.

"We can set aside time for that. Someone in this manor has to agree this is too weird."

I held out my hand for hers. A soft cawing caught my attention as she slipped her hand into mine. Two crows sat in the tree outside my window. Turning back to Blair, I pulled her into my lap.

"Can I kiss you again?"

"Why?" she asked, and a gentle smile curved my mouth. I liked this game she'd started.

"Because I'm tired of this manor and I need to taste you again," I whispered against her lips. She was lovely, and with each brush of contact, my heart soared.

"But what about Aspendale?" Her hands moved through my hair and a shiver went down my spine when her nails grazed my scalp.

"Tomorrow, we'll find him tomorrow. I need to have you now, Blair." I moved her hips, letting her feel the hardness of my cock between her legs. Her eyes searched mine as she moved over my lap with the best torture.

"And if I don't let you kiss me, what happens?" She trailed her nose along mine.

"I ask tomorrow and hope for a new answer."

"A whole day?" She kept edging me.

"Blair," I whispered into her mouth, vying for a kiss to end my agony. My hands traveled up her hips and back until they cradled her face. "I need you. Let me have you, please. I've missed the taste of you."

"Fuck me, Heath."

"Is it still okay that we don't have condoms?"

"Yes, I have an IUD," she said sweetly.

I was on her in an instant. I picked her up and walked to the bed. Her breath was mine and I wasn't leaving her touch for anything. She unbuttoned my shirt and trailed her fingers over my chest. I laid her on my bed and kissed down her neck. With each button I unfastened, I planted a kiss on her exposed flesh.

"I could eat you," I said, biting her breast and leaving another purple mark on her smooth skin.

"Please do," she cried, writhing beneath me.

Unzipping her skirt, I took in the disheveled woman beneath me. Her skin was flushed and bruised, a beautiful sight. I kept her heels on for the moment—the little fasteners would drive me insane to get off and I craved her now.

She wore a silky black pair of lace underwear, and while I wanted to rip them off, I slid them down with care. I grabbed her hips and licked through her wetness. My hand had been here, but this was so much better. Her clit swelled as I licked and sucked. Blair dug her nails into my shoulders as she bucked.

"Heath, I'm . . ." Her panting picked up. I pushed two fingers into her soaked pussy, feeling her clench around me as I stroked.

"So beautiful when you come for me," I finished for her. Blair arched off the bed and begged for more. I sat up and stripped down. Crawling over her, I kissed up her body and left small, reddened bruises. "What's your safeword?" I whispered in her ear.

"I don't know. Can you make it?"

"Choose a word, Blair," I instructed her. I wouldn't touch her further without one. "I want to hurt you in the best ways, but I need you safe."

"I-I don't . . . Crow. The word is crow."

"My macabre love." I reached my hand down between us and guided the head of my cock into her slick, tight pussy. "You feel so good," I whispered across her cheek. I let my arm frame her head, and my fingers slid into her dark waves. I fucked her hard, letting all the pent-up desire I had consume me. Consume us.

I brought my other hand to her throat, squeezing and watching her face flush red. She gasped as I rutted into her deeper. Her eyes were wide and wet with tears.

"Crow," she rasped, and I released her immediately and withdrew. I flipped her over, trailing my hands over her backside.

"Is that for everything?" I asked, kissing her soft shoulder.

"No, sir. I want more."

She moved onto her knees, and I propped her hips up high. Giving her a moment to recover, I parted her with my tongue, licking through the mess I'd made of her and tasting every ounce of her sweet arousal.

"Heath, please," she begged. I licked up and over her ass.

I'd claim every inch of her. My hand came down on her pale flesh, marking it and turning it pink with my handprint. Again. Again. She cried out, shivering as a wave of pleasure coursed through her. Her ass was a polite shade of red, and with one more pop, it turned crimson.

I gripped her hips—they were sure to bruise—and I buried myself inside her. The sound of her ass against me spurred me on faster. I grabbed her by the neck and pulled her against me as I fought my own release.

"You're exquisite, little one."

I pushed her flush to the mattress and adjusted her leg as I rutted into her. She screamed, earth-shatteringly so, before she was a twitching mess of incoherent rambles beneath me. I wanted more from her, craved to take and take—wring out every last bit of lust swirling inside her.

Her body gave out, and I took a moment to face her my way.

"Hey, you're doing so good for me, Blair," I said, softly stroking her face. She nodded and whimpered. "Keep going?"

"Yes, sir."

Pinning her knees, I kept it slow and deep. Her abdomen rolled with each wave as I brought her closer. My release approached, but I needed one more from her.

"You're mine now. You understand that, right?"

Warmth worked its way up my back and my hips stuttered as her pussy clenched around me.

"Yes, sir. I'm yours." I was on her in an instant, kissing her as my cum filled her tight cunt.

"Mine."

"Yours," she affirmed. I rolled us onto our sides and kept her tucked into my chest.

"Mine, all mine."

NINE
AS THE CROWS CAW

HEATH

BLAIR HAD STAYED, and we were in my bed, working late on our assumptions. I bent down to kiss her head as she sat between my legs. She worked on her computer, and I read through a textbook while mentally taking notes. Crows cawed outside. Once, twice, three times. They were loud and constant. Blair yawned, and thunder rolled in the distance.

"Sleepy, little crow?" She looked up at me, her brow pinched as her mind turned. We hadn't discussed anything about us and we were long overdue for it.

"A bit."

"You're welcome to sleep over." She smiled, her face lighting up as her mouth opened. She was interrupted by a crack of thunder and the flicker of lights.

"It storms a lot. Have you noticed?"

"Part of the charm, I suppose. So, do you want to spend the night with me?" She thought it over, watching me before her eyes shifted somewhere else. I was content to wait for her answer, but screams moved across the courtyard, growing faint before disappearing altogether.

We sat up, looking at each other and then to the window.

"That's the west wing again," I said, shifting out from under Blair. She followed me to the window. It was too dark to make anything out below.

"We need to go down there," Blair whispered. "We need to see for ourselves before it's covered up. But how do we avoid Cressida?"

"She should be asleep, no? We'll go down there, look for anything we can find, and leave behind nothing. In and out like we weren't even there."

Blair's hand moved through her hair as she twisted it into a bun before securing it. "Let's go then," she said, grinning with mischief.

After grabbing a flashlight and making our way to the west wing doors, I stopped Blair.

"It doesn't matter what we find, we touch nothing and do nothing," I whispered. Her eyes searched mine.

"I understand," she said, nodding.

"We'll start on the first floor and go up. Clarice was on the first floor, so maybe there's a pattern. Under no circumstances are you to leave my side." She nodded again.

The hallway was eerily silent. Two interns to a floor meant that there was only one left. The first door was wide open, and the room was empty with the bare minimum essentials we were all given. I turned back to Blair, nodding toward the room.

"Clarice," I whispered. We kept our slow pace as we approached the second room at the end of the hall. The door was cracked and entirely dark.

Peeking inside, I saw the gruesome scene of an intern named Renee in her bed, eviscerated. Blood sprayed in every direction from the bed. .

"You don't want to see that," I whispered to Blair. "That's no accident, and it'll never pass for suicide. This was intentional and with motive."

"But what motive could there be for this?" she

asked in hushed tones as we walked back to the east wing.

"I'm not sure, but we'll figure it out. I'll write it all down in my notes and see how the story changes over time." The sound of high heels pierced the air as we walked down the hall. Recognizing Cressida's steps, I pulled Blair into Clarice's old room. She looked fearful as Cressida approached. I covered Blair's mouth with my hand and waited as she stopped just shy of the door.

The silence was loud, and I held my breath, cursing years of smoking and how it made my lungs ache. We didn't move or twitch an eye as nervous sweat beaded my brow. Her heels continued to click down the corridor, and we released sighs of relief.

"Not yet," I whispered as Cressida made it down the hall and turned around. Her steps faded past the room, and I released Blair.

"Do you think she knows?"

"Only time will tell, but I'm more curious about what she's going to do about this one." I peeked out of the room. "We need to go," I said, pulling her by the hand and running through the annex and back to the east wing.

THE SUN CAME through the window and the warmth on my face stirred me awake. Blair was on my chest, and she groaned as I moved to get up.

"I don't want to go," she whined. Her voice was thick and husky in the morning; it made me want to crawl back in bed and ravage her.

"Sleep then. I'm going to get dressed." The clock tower chimed seven times, and she cracked her eyes open while wearing a massive frown. As I walked to the closet, I noted four crows collecting on my windowsill.

How many crows make a murder? More than one in general?

I dressed in a simple button-down and slacks, opting for a cozy sweater when it got too cold. When I stepped out, Blair was up and moving.

"Your turn, dear." I led her down the hall to her room, where I sat on her bed while she rummaged through her closet.

"What do you think of this?" she said, walking out in a gorgeous black dress and oversized cardigan.

"It looks beautiful on you," I said, mesmerized by her. My hand itched to draw her like this. I also had the urge to strip her down and sleep in today. But it was a new week. *I can't...*

"These shoes?" She stepped out again and did a turn to show them off, and I nodded my head. Blood was rushing somewhere else, and I fought to keep the lust at bay.

"Come here," I said gently. She came to me, and I pulled her into a light kiss, enough to satisfy me for the time being. "You're perfection," I whispered against her lips.

She shook me off and went to the bathroom where she did her normal makeup. When she was ready, I took her arm in mine and led her out.

She looked ahead and was talking about something, but I was enraptured and couldn't stop staring.

That was, until her face twisted and a piercing scream hit my ears. I looked in the direction she did on the stairs and instinctively grabbed her. I saw it then, the body hanging in the stairwell. I shielded her view and pulled out my phone, but there was no signal. I always had service.

I ushered Blair downstairs away from the horrific scene. She muttered to herself as tears started to fall over her cheeks. I sat her down and turned and saw Cressida talking to a man I recognized as the sketchy coroner from days prior.

"Cressida," I barked more harshly than I'd intended, but I was fed up. She looked over, taken aback. "Another intern is on the stairs in the east wing."

"Mr. Crowley," she started to chastise me, but I scooped up Blair and ignored her as I made our way to the library.

BLAIR

Heath had gone back for our envelopes when I'd calmed down, but I didn't see the point. People were dying and we were supposed to carry on like nothing had happened, or would continue to happen, in this case. It was apparent these weren't supernatural causes.

I walked the aisles of old medical texts and thought over any possible motives. A chill came at my back, and I turned around to see a swirling mass of darkness taking shape. I expected to see a demonic Heath again, but the apparition that formed in front of me looked different. He was a younger man, and I couldn't quite place the familiarity.

"Who are you?" I whispered, stepping back and getting ready to run.

"You haven't figured it out yet, have you? You will soon. I'll see to it." His voice was deep and distorted.

"Why are you killing people?" The figure moved closer.

"Why do you think I am? Why won't you help me? I brought you here to help me!" He reached out for my hand. The ring on my finger burned hot and I shouted from the pain.

The figure disappeared as Heath's footsteps approached. He rushed around the corner and took me in his arms, looking me over. I winced when he grabbed my hand, and his touch became gentle.

"I heard you yell; are you okay?" I nodded and explained the experience, and he got hung up on the same detail I had. "Brought you here, what does that mean?"

"We need to speak to Dr. Aspendale. This has gone on long enough, and between the haunting and the murders, I'm ready to go home." Heath nodded and we started to leave. Looking up, I felt uneasy. The crows were coming like omens. A single one sat in each of the five overhead windows. A shiver worked down my spine.

"Oh, wait here. I left my sweater." He took off before I could say anything, and I stood by the doors. Dread filled me and I wanted to leave. A familiar creaking noise filled the air, like wood ready to snap.

I stood straighter and watched as a book stack toppled to the floor.

"Heath!" I called out. I heard a shout and just before the crash, I saw that stark white-blond hair move. He was feet away from the destruction, panting.

"We can leave now."

TEN
SIX IS A MURDER

BLAIR

"SHE WASN'T receptive to our first inquiry; why would she entertain us now?" I asked Heath as he threw a cardigan on. He ran his hands through his still damp hair.

"I doubt she will, but it'll give us answers regardless." He grabbed a few things from his desk and walked across the room to his open door. "After you," he said as he motioned his hands.

We didn't talk as we walked down the stairs and into the annex. Truth be told, I was still rattled from the man's proclaimed suicide in the stairwell. It was quiet and had been increasingly so since the murders had become more frequent. The authorities claimed they were accidents; only Heath and I referred to them as murders in private.

I felt a chill as we walked down the hall toward Cressida's office. I looked around, noting that behind us, the apparition had appeared once again. No one seemed to notice, not even Heath. By the time I blinked, he was gone. There was a pull toward the spirit when he wasn't being a menace. A familiarity of sorts that I couldn't place.

Heath knocked on Cressida's door, and when she called in response, he looked at me and offered a nod of encouragement.

Inside her sterile office, unease set in.

"You two again. How can I help you?" she asked, looking between us.

"We'd like to speak to Dr. Aspendale, and we were wondering if you could set up a meeting," I said, hesitant to reveal too much.

"Is this about our previous discussion?" Her eyes narrowed, and I almost caved under her intense, sharp scrutiny.

"No, ma'am. This is about the internship and getting clearer information on the end goal." Heat moved up my spine with the lie and sweat moistened the back of my neck.

"Dr. Aspendale is an incredibly busy man, Ms. Grimm. I can assure you any questions you have can be brought to me and I'll pass them along. If you have any needs, I'll also send them to him for approval. It's a busy week. You two need to get back to work."

Just like that, she'd shut us down again. Her attention went down to her paperwork in a final, unspoken dismissal.

Heath stood first and I followed him. Her door shut softly, and I turned to face him.

"That was helpful?" I whispered as we walked through the annex. He stopped at the board and collected our tasks.

"It was a start," he whispered, leaning in close. "She's hiding something and she wants us away from Aspendale. She's wedging herself into that space and I want to know why." He grinned, licking his lip before drawing it between his teeth.

He moved forward, mouth primed to say something, when he was cut off by screams. An intern ran down the stairs, looking behind him.

"Ghosts! The manor is haunted!" He screamed louder and louder as he stumbled through the annex. Cressida's office door opened and she stepped out to observe the scene.

The man continued to scream until he clutched his chest in pained silence. He struggled to make sounds before falling over and struggling to breathe. Heath and I rushed to his side, but Cressida backed us off.

"Leave, go." I wanted to protest her callousness, but Heath pulled my arm and led me toward the east wing.

"WHAT DO you think Cressida will say about this one?" Heath asked as I peered out the window. I watched the asylum as crows gathered on its rooftop. Six little crows sat in a line and peered below.

"Scared to death by heart attack is my bet," I said with distraction. "I wanna go to the asylum." It called to me. Something about its presence today was telling and I wanted to listen.

"The asylum? Are you sure?" I nodded, unable to take my eyes off the building. I heard Heath move behind me.

"Positive."

"Let's go tonight," he offered. A hand trailed up my arm and over my shoulder before resting against my neck. "If that's what you want to do," he whispered, "we'll do it." A gentle kiss was pressed to my temple and then cold set in behind me as he stepped away.

I looked over my shoulder and watched as Heath went to his closet and pulled out a small book bag. He walked to his desk and grabbed a book; I noticed it was one of the ones he'd offered to me to read. Heath stopped, poked through a few notebooks, and added them to his handful.

"Have we said fuck it to the tasks?" he asked, a sly grin pulling at the corners of his mouth.

"If not, we're close to it."

"Do you need convincing?" He looked up from his bag, his eyebrow arched.

"I feel our methods of persuasion differ." He rummaged through a side table drawer and pulled out a flashlight that he tossed in with the other items. He walked up to me then, hands gently cradling my face.

"How right you are, dear." Heath kissed me once, twice, three times. "I doubt the work matters much with this madness going on." Another series of small, drawing kisses. Words were hollow and thoughts were sparse. I just wanted him to keep kissing me. "Say fuck it."

"Fuck me," I whispered.

"That'll do." His touch intensified as his tongue snaked into my mouth. His hands on my face kept my mouth open as his tongue explored. I was a captive when he kissed me. Unable to free myself, not that I wanted to be anywhere else except in his arms. He had complete control over me.

Heath released my face, and I crossed my arms over his shoulders. He grasped my ass, cold fingers grazing beneath my skirt.

"Do you have to wear these skirts all the time? They're killing me." He groaned, taking my lip between his teeth.

"Then they're doing their job."

He pulled me flush against his body and I whimpered with the contact. I needed to be under him. On top of him. I wanted to be consumed by him.

"You're so distracting, Ms. Blair."

"You still have restraint left, Mr. Crowley." He hooked a hand beneath my knee and wrapped my leg around his waist.

"I want you just like this when we get back." He peered down at me. My chest brushed his as my breaths came quick and deep. "Go change," he instructed.

WE STOOD on the path in front of the steps of the asylum. Heath looked around, but my mind was elsewhere. I was back in his room—back in his arms.

"What's that?" Heath asked, the flashlight moving back and forth on the steps. "It's shiny," he muttered, stepping forward and bending down. I walked up behind him, trying to see what he reached for. His arm stopped moving and he reached into his bag, pulling out a tissue.

"What is it?" I squinted over his shoulder.

"This, dear, is a gold tooth." His light illuminated the gold-capped tooth he held. It looked bloody at the root, almost like it had been forcibly removed.

"That, love, is gross," I retorted as he set it inside a plastic bag and tucked it away. He laughed and stood fully. When he walked up the steps and into the facility, I followed.

It was . . . old. Decrepit. We walked into a time capsule of dust and cobwebs. A wheelchair sat in the middle of the lobby and it, too, was covered in decades of grime and rust.

"How long has this place been abandoned?" I wondered out loud. Heath took it seriously and responded.

"Over fifty years." His voice was low and calm as

he searched with his flashlight. He pointed it toward a set of doors. "Through there?" he asked. I nodded and followed him, the squeal of the doors almost unbearable. "What exactly are we here to find?"

"I don't know," I answered honestly. "It was just a feeling." It was even less than a hunch. The tooth was a surprising find, but I didn't know what had drawn me here. It was eerie, rundown, and hardly worth anything.

We passed a room and I turned, feeling something creep up my spine. I reached out and looked back to Heath.

"Hey—ouch!" I looked down. Instead of grabbing the doorknob, I'd been distracted with getting his attention and had cut my hand on the broken glass in the small window beside the handle.

"You okay?" Heath rushed to my side and covered my palm with his, bringing it above my head. He was much taller, and I ended up partially on my tiptoes.

"I'll be okay," I said as I felt blood trickle down my forearm. The scent of iron filled the air between us. "I just need it to stop bleeding."

"Keep the pressure," he instructed me as he let my hand go.

He unbuttoned his dress shirt and ripped his

undershirt. Blood stained his white clothing. Heath wrapped the shirt around my hand and tied it off. I felt the thump of pulse, but the rivulets of blood stopped. This would require a trip to the infirmary when we got back.

"We can go—"

"No, we stay. I felt something when we passed by that room." Heath walked past me and dusted off the plaque.

"Dr. Aspendale," he read off. "This must have been his father's office." Opening the door, we stepped inside. It was a typical office, but it looked like it'd been abandoned in the middle of a workday.

Something in the air stirred, and I felt a cold draft behind me.

"Heath," I whispered, too afraid to move.

"Yeah," he started as he turned around. He paused, his face in shock as he looked at me. No, he looked past me. "Blair."

"I feel it."

"I *see* it," he said through gritted teeth. I stepped forward as Heath opened his arms for me. Turning, I saw the same apparition as before.

"Who are you?" I asked, but it gave me no response.

"Why are you haunting her? Why are you here?"

Heath questioned. The apparition looked at him and raised a hand to point at me.

"She has something of mine," it said. The apparition didn't seem to care that I was standing here now.

"Why can I see you?"

"You took something of mine as well." He pointed at Heath now. His ghostly body started to fade in and out.

"Who are you?" I asked again, and finally the apparition looked at me.

"Find my body. Let me rest." This was a twist. It had been acting out because it was trapped in the manor.

But who was he?

"Let's go, Blair." Heath pulled at my elbow and as we left, I looked behind us. The man appeared on the steps, his face pained as he watched us retreat.

"Heath . . ."

"I don't know, but we'll figure it out," he answered.

ELEVEN
SECRETS TO BE HELD

BLAIR

THE PRINTER WHIRRED AS MORE pages came out. I picked them up from the tray and pieced them together on my wall using pins. We constructed a board for the web of information we were uncovering. Heath could work off memory, but I couldn't.

I wrote the dates of the interns' deaths under their pictures and put them into chronological order. We were down to six alive and six deceased. This place was a nightmare and there was no predicting what was to come. Most of the deaths had been thought to be natural occurrences or suicides, but when I thought about the events from earlier,

Heath's in the library had been outright attempted murder.

"Little crow," he whispered by my ear. His arms came around my waist. With his head on my shoulder, he sighed. "You've been at this for hours."

"I know, I'm almost done." I pinned a list of events under his name and photo. "I was just thinking about you, actually."

"Oh yeah?"

"Maybe not in the fondest way, but I realized that of the interns that have already died, each can be attributed to either a natural death or a suicide. If we're to believe the reports, that is." I tapped his photo. "But for you, it was an outright attempted murder. Why is that?"

"That's a good question," he said, kissing across my shoulder and up the side of my neck. "But let's answer it at a later date." His kisses turned to bites. Slowly, he started to suck my flesh between his teeth.

"And what"—I moaned as he deepened the pull—"are we going to do instead?" His hands moved across my abdomen as he undressed me.

"I'm sure we can occupy ourselves with something, dear Blair." I turned into his hold and met his lips. A deep, slow kiss stole me away from my task.

My fingers worked the buttons of his shirt as he walked me back to the bed.

He picked me up effortlessly and laid me down, sliding my thong off and tossing it across the room. He kissed up my thighs, and I ran my fingers through his hair. Heath slid his tongue through my center and I melted into the bed. He licked and nipped, sucked and worshiped my pussy.

"Heath," I called out.

My grip in his hair tightened. He hummed against my flesh, but no real answer to his name formed. My thighs squeezed him as my orgasm crested. I pushed him back until he got the hint. His eyebrow raised slightly.

"Lie down," I instructed. He tugged his pants and boxers off.

His cock was large and throbbing in my hand. With gentle strokes, I glided up and down his shaft before licking the head of his cock. He was velvety smooth and delicious on my tongue. I took him into my mouth fully and he groaned. Heath laced his fingers through my hair and controlled the movement of my head.

"Fuck, Blair..."

He groaned as he hit the back of my throat. I wanted his release, but I wanted him to come inside me more. I audibly popped off his cock and watched as his chest heaved.

"Thank fuck," he said breathlessly. "I was going to come if you kept that up, and I really, really want to lose myself inside you."

I crawled over him and settled my knees beside his hips. He reached down and helped me get situated. I slowly eased my way down his cock, watching his abdomen tighten every time I went deeper.

"Blair, love, you can't do this to me." His hands found my hips and he tried to make me go down fully, though it was more of a half-hearted attempt. "Please," he begged. I continued to take him little by little. "Please, little crow."

I slammed my hips down, feeling him hard against my deepest wall. It took my breath and his. Rolling his hips, he matched his thrusts. Sweat dripped down my back as I worked his cock inside me. I tensed as he coaxed an orgasm forward. His thumb was rough against my clit.

"Heath, I'm—"

"I know, baby."

I planted my hands on his chest before I could fall forward. My hips jerked and my thighs shook as I rode out my orgasm. He felt so good inside me, I didn't want to stop.

"Blair," he whispered.

I felt it then, the twitch of his cock in time with the pulse of each wave of mine. Hot cum filled me and he groaned as I kept going, well beyond my spent limit. I didn't want to stop.

"Come here." He pulled me close, slipping out and leaving me to writhe against nothing. He kissed me deeply and his hand wrapped around my throat. "You have the greediest cunt. I love it."

TWELVE
WISHFUL THINKING

HEATH

"TODAY IS INVESTIGATION DAY," I said, tugging on Blair's ankle. She groaned and stirred in the sheets. I'd learned quickly she wasn't the happiest morning person.

"Later," she murmured before tucking into the sheets deeper.

"I already let you sleep later, come on." I pulled her by the ankle halfway down the bed and kissed up her leg. "We need to find Aspendale and get to the bottom of this."

"Fine," she grumbled before turning and rolling

out. Her steps were heavy and full of sass as she walked to my bathroom.

While she showered, I pulled out my notebook and sketched a few more poses of Blair. Her face was always full of emotion. She was perfect.

When the water turned off, I closed the book and dropped it back into a desk drawer for later. She stepped out in a towel and winked at me as she crossed my room and slipped out into the hallway, carefully closing the door behind her. I chuckled to myself and decided to follow suit as I got dressed.

"WHERE DO WE START?" Blair asked as she slid her spoon around the edge of her yogurt cup.

"Let's just go to the source. His office is listed in the directory; I saw it when I got here." I took a bite of my granola bar.

"Do you remember where it's at?"

"Of course, I do," I said, shocked she'd even have to ask. "His office is on the records hall, just a bit farther than where we went." She nodded, silently eating her yogurt. Contemplation rippled over her face. "What are you thinking about?"

"Bad omens."

"That's not ominous." I watched as her brows pinched together.

"Have you noticed that every time we see crows, something happens?" I smiled at her.

"Well then, it's a good thing I didn't see any crows today." She shook her head and tossed her yogurt cup in a nearby trash bin.

"I did. When I was in my room this morning getting dressed." She waved a hand through the air in dismissal. "It's probably nothing, I'm just paranoid after everything that's happened. Forget I mentioned it."

"Forgotten," I said, but I wouldn't forget, not where Blair's discomfort was concerned. If I could convince her to believe in ghosts, I could believe in her bad omens.

We made our way to the records hall without incident. There'd been a lull in the deaths since the other night. We weren't sure if the failed attempt on our lives had disrupted the plan, but we were thankful for it. Of the remaining interns, only a couple had decided to show up for any work.

"There it is," Blair whispered as she wiped off the dusty name plaque by the door. "Why . . . ?"

"What is it?"

"Why would that be dusty?" She looked up at

me, her thumb and finger rubbing the dust off her hand.

"Add it to the list of shit we don't yet understand." I knocked on Aspendale's door and we waited.

There was nothing—no movement, no sounds, no greeting. We looked at each other, puzzled and concerned. Blair knocked this time, but it was the same result. I held up a finger to stall her on any outbursts. Gently, I turned the doorknob. It gave way easily enough and I peeked inside.

"Blair," I whispered. "No one's here." We stepped inside and closed the door behind us.

"Why would Cressida say he's here and working if no one has stepped foot in this office for quite some time?" Blair looked around and stopped abruptly.

"What is it?" I asked when she rushed to the wall with photo frames. She grabbed one, and I walked over, peering over her shoulder.

"That's the man," she whispered. In the frame was an old picture of a young man and woman holding a baby. She leaned in closer and looked at her hand. "And that's . . . my ring?"

"What?" I asked, moving closer to the photo. Sure enough, the woman in the photo wore the same ring that sat on Blair's middle finger. Her hands moved fast, grabbing the photo and turning it around.

Norman Aspendale, Judith Richardson, Loren "Rory" Richardson

Blair's mouth moved with each name silently passing her lips. Her hands shook.

I slipped the photo from her grasp and turned her to me.

"Hey," I said calmly. My voice was a gentle rasp.

"Hey," she choked out.

"It's okay. Tell me what's going on."

She looked at the photo in my hands, her face a mix of horror and shock. Unblinking, she said, "That's my mother. That's my adoptive mother. Loren."

I inspected the photo. "We'll figure it out," I promised. It was becoming a habitual thing to promise, but if it was the last thing I did, I'd make sense of all this. "First, we need to go through this office. I doubt anyone is coming by soon, so we can take our time."

I reached out and set the photo on the end table. She took steadying breaths and closed her eyes.

"Okay," she said firmly. "Okay. We can make sense of this." She turned on her heel and walked over to the desk to rummage through drawers.

"We can talk at the same time if you need—"

The slam of a drawer cut me off.

"She never mentioned Aspendale. Why? Why would they lie to me about my grandfather?" She crossed her arms and sat back in the chair. "They always said my grandfather died when my mother was young. Why keep him a secret?"

"A baby out of wedlock in that time period? It's understandable. I take it your dad . . ." I didn't feel like much help.

"He's alive, Theodore Grimm. But he never mentioned Grandma Richardson's family either. He probably doesn't know."

"You said you were adopted, right?"

"Yes," she started, but I didn't finish my thought. I jumped into action and started going through Aspendale's desk rapidly. "What if he knew about you?"

My mind raced with thoughts and theories that I couldn't put into words right away.

"I brought you here," she said, voicing the connection that I'd made.

"So, Aspendale is haunting the manor . . ."

"That means he's dead," she said in horror.

"And that Cressida is a liar."

Time passed as I demolished Aspendale's office.

Blair sat in the chair, and at one point she'd asked for the photo again. She'd stared at it as I'd searched for anything that'd give us an answer.

"I've found nothing," I said, defeated and sweaty. I faced the wall of frames. *What secrets are you hiding, old man?*

It didn't stand out initially, but the more I stared, the more the center frame looked out of place. It wasn't by design or decoration, but its pronounced face along the wall. With a gentle finger, I tugged the bottom corner and it opened like a small door. A safe sat in the depression.

"Blair," I whispered.

"I see it," she answered. The chair scratched across the hardwood as she stood. "Put my grandmother's birthday in. 0-6-2-8."

The numbers beeped as I typed them into the keypad. After a series of rapid beeps, the light turned green and the safe popped open.

"Holy shit," I said. There was a leather journal sitting on a stack of file folders. "That's it," I whispered, carefully pulling the journal out and laying it on the side table. "Here, go through these," I instructed, passing off the folders to Blair.

I flipped through the pages in the journal, catching various anecdotes over years. I stopped when I read a familiar name. These entries were about Blair's grandmother and, multiple times over, Aspendale's wishes that they could be together.

My Judith is pregnant. She says the baby will be a girl and she's going to name her Loren. It's a beautiful name. I'm going to be a dad. How can one call himself a father if he's not going to be present? Judith said these were matters for another time. We're having a baby.

I flipped through more of the journal and collected more stories about him, Judith, and Loren. Some entries were about loss, and others were births or marriages, like Loren and Theodore's. I stopped at an entry dated the year Blair was born. I read through that year slowly.

Judith tells me Loren and Theo are unable to have children.
They're trying IVF.
They've decided to adopt.
My granddaughter is home. Her name is Blair Grimm. She's a beautiful little thing. I've decided to leave it all to her.

"Blair." My voice came out hoarse. She looked

up from her files. Her big brown eyes were round and wondering. "You're..."

"What is it?" she asked, standing and walking around his desk. Her hand was soft on my elbow.

"We have to find the official paperwork for his claims, but you're the heir to the Aspendale Estate. He knew about you, Blair. He says it right here," I explained, pointing to the entry where her name is underlined.

"I don't..." She took the journal and read over it herself, her fingers trailing down the ink as her eyes welled with tears. She got lost in the journal, and I walked around the desk, grabbing the next file and flipping through it with no time to waste.

I opened the fourth—his will.

"Blair, I found it. I found everything." There was too much going on to process everything. "Okay, let's take a pause. What are the odds anyone else knows about this?" I asked, holding the file up.

"I don't think anyone does, honestly." Blair chewed on her lip, as I waited for her to finish. "If you think about it, we're of the belief Aspendale—my grandfather, mind you—is haunting the estate, which means he's dead. Everyone else thinks he's alive and they're doing intern work for him."

"We need to connect this all; it's hurting my

head." I organized the files from the safe and put them back. Turning to Blair and nodding to the journal, I asked, "Do you want to keep that?"

"Is it too much of an ask?"

"Not at all."

"Then I'd like to keep it," she said, hugging it close to her chest.

"I will caution you, don't let it out of your sight. Remember those books you borrowed?" She nodded. "Remember the passage about objects and the deceased? This could mean more Aspendale sightings and hauntings."

"I remember. I'm okay with that now."

I cleaned the office, placing everything back where I could remember it being.

"So, Blair?" I asked, and she looked up at me. "Do you believe in ghosts now?"

THIRTEEN
ALL QUESTIONS, NO ANSWERS

BLAIR

HEATH'S HEART thumped under my head and his chest rose with each breath, moving my focus a few inches every time. I sat up and looked down at him.

"It's been quiet," I said pointedly. "There have been no murders and Aspendale has been silent. Or, well, absent I should say."

"Have you tried to reach out to him like that book I gave you said to?" I shook my head.

"I'm a chicken," I admitted. "I used to not believe in these things, but here we are, and it's already a lot to process on top of the granddaughter thing."

"I understand. We can try together if you'd like."

"I would," I said, turning and rolling out of my bed.

I looked at the wall we'd pieced together earlier, but it wasn't as accurate or complete as it could be.

"We know Aspendale is dead," I said matter-of-factly. "But we don't know if it was natural or another homicide."

"Yes, and if that was rhetorical, then you can tell me to shut up." I laughed him off; he was welcome to speak whenever he wanted. "The hard part is piecing together a motive."

"Well, what are the common motives for murder?"

"Love, money, and some third thing I'm sure." I grinned and pulled out my phone to search for it myself. "It says here lust, love, loathing, and loot."

"I feel like we can rule a few things out, honestly. When it comes down to it, Aspendale was suspected of having no children. I'd say money fits the bill."

"Do we know who benefits without a will?"

"We can make assumptions," he said, sighing and running a hand through his hair.

"Let's update this board," I said, printing off more papers. I pinned them in place, and Heath read over my shoulder. "Which of these could be a ghost murder?"

"I'd say these," he said as he tapped three photos. "This is too horrific, this is too passionate, and this one was self-inflicted, so I'd rule those out."

"Could they also be murders?"

"Unfortunately, yes. The only way to know is to believe what Aspendale tells you the next time you see him appear."

"This is really morbid," I said as I moved the group of remaining interns. "But we need to determine who could be next."

"Not to brag, but I've almost died twice now," Heath said, putting a hand to his chest as he grinned.

"And I was with you," I reminded him. "We don't know if others have had multiple attempts on their lives, so with our limited knowledge, let's move us to the front."

We went back and forth on the other interns, throwing out plausible reasons until finally we decided on an order that made sense to both of us.

"I don't think I like leading this one," Heath mused as he gazed at the board.

"I'm not a fan either, but it's the reality we're in." I moved pictures around, but Heath remained silent as he watched me move my photo under Aspendale's.

"What's that for, love?"

"We forgot about motive," I whispered. "Whoever is after Aspendale's estate or money, whatever the reason, the means would be to get rid of me."

"If they know about you," he said gently, as though that possibility would soothe anything. Of course they knew.

"I doubt I'd be here if they didn't. This feels like a ruse."

"Who has the means to set that up?"

"The million-dollar question."

FOURTEEN
SIX, SEVEN, EIGHT LITTLE CROWS

BLAIR

I'D NEVER BEEN *good about discerning when I was dreaming, but this was one of those undeniable times. I watched as time was both fast and slow, faces I knew and those I didn't blurring together. There was a jumbled series of events that made no sense, and the more it went on, the more it devolved. I turned away from the madness; it was loud and everywhere. I walked toward the darkness of my mind for some reprieve.*

What followed me were footsteps. I lowered my hands from my ears and faced the sound. Nothing. Nothing accompanied the sound, but I heard them move closer. Starting at the feet, an apparition slowly revealed itself in front of me.

"Aspendale," I breathed. My voice was distorted a bit.

"You know, Blair. You know."

"I do," I said, assuming he meant what we'd found in his office. He shook his head, and the movement shifted his appearance in a blur of motion almost too fast for me to keep up with the finer details of his face.

"In the asylum. You know, Blair. You could feel it. Go there today. Help me, Blair."

"I don't know how," I said, desperation lacing my words as my heart sank.

"You will."

Aspendale's hand reached out, and I thought he was asking me to take it, but then I felt a blast in my chest that threw me back into the deep, deep darkness.

I woke, startled and screaming as my mind discerned the dream darkness from the room's. What echoed my scream was the sound of death on another floor.

"Blair," Heath said beside me. I looked over, and worry was etched into his crinkled brow. "You've been screaming for some time now; I couldn't wake you up."

"Aspendale," I whispered. "He was in my dream. He came to me. He said, he said . . ." I tried to bring back the conversation from just a moment before. "The asylum, I have to help him in the asylum."

Another scream pierced the air, and it chilled me to the bone.

"We have to go to the asylum today." I looked at the murder board we'd started. "And someone needs to be moved."

By morning, Heath and I were dressed and downstairs before the final bell could toll. We watched the coroner, who suspiciously wasn't a proper coroner, wheel out another body. I counted the faces in the room with us, stopping when I saw Cressida. She had a hand over her heart, shaking her head in disbelief. Or rather, what she wanted to appear as disbelief.

"Upstairs," I whispered to Heath. We slipped out of the annex and back into the stairwell as we hurried back to my room.

He held the door open for me, and I walked inside and made a beeline for the board. I picked up the third photo in our potential list and moved her to the other side.

"An overdose, but we heard her screaming for

her life." Heath dropped onto my bed, and I sat beside him.

"I'll be honest, the attention split between these murders and the haunting is doing them both a disservice," I said, sighing as I took in the board. "If we go off another assumption, Aspendale was the first death. They're all linked, so finding Aspendale and solving his murder is the answer to solving the others."

"How confident are you that we can stop them in time to save anyone?" Heath looked at me then, and I searched his eyes for any hope that I could steal and cling to. I found none.

"I'm a forensic psychologist, not a detective. I don't know how to stop any of this, and I don't know how to solve anything. I can't save anyone, and it terrifies me that I'm part of that list. All we can do is try, Heath."

"That's enough for me. Let's search the asylum."

THE ASYLUM WAS WASHED in the warm glow of the setting sun as we ran inside. Nothing had been disturbed since our first time investigating the place.

We were running out of people who could become nosy. *What a morbid thought . . .*

"Aspendale!" I called out, but no one answered and he made no appearance. We roved our flashlights over the rooms as we searched one by one. "Aspendale, I'm here like you told me to be! Please, help me understand!"

Nothing.

"Do you have the journal?" Heath asked from behind me.

"Yeah, it's in my bag," I said, digging around before my hand found the leather journal and plucked it out. I waved the flashlight over the front so he could see the branded logo sticking out, and I noted it was the number eight and a picture of a crow. How fitting for these times.

"Read from it," he suggested.

"You think that'll get him to show?"

"Anything is worth a shot."

I flipped through the pages until I came to an entry about Judith.

The woman came back with Mr. Richardson. I'd assumed for some time that she was a relative or caretaker of his, but today she told me her name was Judith Richardson and Mr. Richardson was her father. He was a very sick man, and it made me question my morals that I was happy he'd brought her to me.

I'm enamored by her very being. The smallest things she does to the grandest, there's no difference and I am awestruck. I wish for her to be entangled with—

"Stop!" a voice bellowed through the room. The book slammed closed, and I brought it close to my chest before it could fly from my grasp.

"Show yourself, Aspendale!" I yelled back to the disembodied voice. "Now, or I keep reading! I'm done with these games."

Movement across the room made us turn, and our lights illuminated the apparition of young Norman Aspendale. He was more corporeal than ever before and looked genuinely displeased.

"In there," he grumbled, pointing to a room just down the hall. He vanished like fog dissipating, and I started breathing again.

Turning to Heath, I said, "We are never doing

that again." I put the journal back in my bag and followed him down the corridor.

Heath was the first to enter the room and his arm quickly came up in the doorframe, blocking me and my sight.

"Don't," he warned, but I pushed through anyway. My flashlight landed on the gruesome scene.

A decapitated and mutilated head lay in the middle of the room. I averted my eyes and turned toward the hallway. "What are the odds that's Aspendale?" I heard Heath's steps move closer to the center space.

"High odds. And guess what he's missing," Heath said, and shivers worked through my spine.

"What's that?"

"A tooth."

FIFTEEN
COUNT ALL YOUR WOES

HEATH

SLEEP DIDN'T COME EASILY, if it even came. One minute, I was falling asleep with Blair in my arms, and the next it felt like the sun had risen and I'd had no rest. There were no dreams, just endless thoughts about our discovery.

I stared off at the window as the sun peeked over the sill. There were pieces I'd put together, but I didn't want to voice them just yet. They haunted me. It was a constant loop of information that fit together and felt so obvious. Too obvious.

"Good morning." Blair's voice broke through my

thoughts, and I looked down to see her sleepy face looking up at mine.

"Good morning, dear."

"What's on your mind?" she asked, sitting up and blocking one of the rays that'd been in my face.

"A lot of things, too many," I whispered, leaning into her shoulder and kissing the exposed skin there. She laughed and pulled back. I rested against the mattress and sighed, letting the heaviness leave my body. I heard a thump from my desk, and Blair moved.

"I'll get it," she said, and I closed my eyes. Her steps were soft and quiet across the floorboards. "Heath..."

"Hmm?"

"What are these drawings?" My eyes snapped open and I sat up. My notebook had been put in a drawer for safe keeping. When I looked at Blair, there was a misty spirit behind her.

Aspendale.

A secret journal for a secret notebook.

My heart hammered in my chest as words failed to reach my mouth. My breaths came quicker with each page she turned to.

"Heath?"

"I..." *Am an idiot.* "I drew them." She looked at

me. "You were, are, captivating, and there are times where the image of you is burned into my soul so I draw you from memory."

"You drew me from memory?"

"Yes," I said, cautious with the way this could tip in either direction.

"Show me," she said, handing me the notebook.

She reached behind her and grabbed my bag of drawing pencils and tossed them at me. Blair posed on my desk and watched me. "How much time do you need?"

"This is plenty," I said. "But I could watch you all day. I enjoy doing so."

"Turn around."

"Yes, ma'am."

I let my eyes rove over her body once more before I faced the wall against the bed. I flipped to a clean page and started sketching. She stayed silent and so did I, the only sound in the air my pencil against the paper.

"What part are you on?"

"Your legs," I said as I drew along the curve of her thigh for more definition.

"Are you almost done?"

"Yes," I said quietly, almost a whisper. I was lost in her. I could draw her for hours and still want to draw more of her. This notebook would be full soon and I'd have to start another one.

"Time," she called out, and my hand stopped immediately.

She got off the desk and walked over to me. I turned and handed her the sketch pad. She didn't say a word as she looked over every line.

"This is beautiful," she said when she finally spoke again.

"You're beautiful, that's why."

"Heath, what I meant—"

"I know what you meant, but what I said is true as well." I sat there unmoving as I waited for her overall rejection.

"Keep drawing me, I love seeing me through your eyes."

"You asked what was on my mind," I said, recalling earlier. "The truth is a lot, but also it's mostly you. Always you in some thought or abstract idea. I haven't stopped thinking about you since you looked at me in the hallway on the first day."

"Heath," she started, but I waved her off.

"Darker things are occupying the space where I prefer to keep thoughts of you. We need to resolve some of these connections. We're running out of time and luck. I'm . . ."

"You're what?" she asked, taking my hand in hers and placing my palm on her cheek.

"I'm afraid."

"I understand. I feel that way, too. I don't want to end up haunting this estate." Her smile was gentle and kind.

"I think we start going with the obvious answers and choices. I think we should visit the morgue today."

"The morgue?" she asked.

"Yeah, after they established the asylum and after a few patients' untimely deaths, they created a morgue."

"Brutal," she murmured.

"It's on the nose, but it also makes sense that someone would keep bodies there."

"Let's do it."

The basement of the manor was damp and musty. It was clear this hadn't been a functional morgue for quite some time, but all the same it wasn't abandoned like the asylum had been. Electricity was still connected to the floor, and the lights were the annoying fluorescent type.

"This is it," Blair said, watching the double doors and checking down the hallway one last time.

"It is," I echoed. "Are you ready? I'm not certain

we'll find anything, but on the off chance something is behind those doors, are you?"

"How does one prepare for such a reality?" I left her question in the air between us. I had no answer, and it was unkind to think she could be prepared for another life-altering revelation so quickly after the last.

"Do you want me to go in first?" I asked with my hand pressed against the door. She looked on in silence, likely debating her answer. I took her hesitation as the indication that I should. I wouldn't stop her, but I'd at least be a shield.

I pushed the door open and saw . . . nothing. Not a damn thing looked to be out of place. The tables were neat, clean, and organized. It was like no one had even come down here today save for the lights being turned on.

I looked back at Blair to question my miscalculation, but she shook her head.

"Check the body drawers." I was off my game. Where else would one store a body in a morgue?

We walked to opposite sides and pulled open drawers. I managed the top row while she handled the bottom. They all came up empty. On opposite sides again, we started on the middle row.

"If he's not here, where do we look next?" Door after door, we closed, only cool air to be found inside.

"Graveyard or the asylum?" she suggested. It made sense. His head was found in the wretched place, so why wouldn't the rest—

"Oh." I froze. The center drawer was occupied by a body with a sheet over top of it. I pulled on the slab and rolled it out between us. I didn't bother counting down. This was the moment we couldn't have prepared for.

I drew back the sheet and saw a frightening, disfigured, and mutilated body. He was missing a head, that much I'd anticipated, but more than that he was sectioned and quartered into manageable pieces.

"What the fuck?" Blair exclaimed, averting her gaze and bringing a hand to her mouth. "I'm gonna be sick," she murmured.

"You and me both, love," I affirmed as I analyzed his corpse. An arm and a leg were missing alongside the head. Something else struck me as odd.

"Who does this?"

"A sick, sick individual." I covered up his body once more and pushed the slab back into the cooler. "Another thing to add to our list of mysteries, where are his clothes?"

SIXTEEN
THE ROAD MAP SO FAR

BLAIR

I STOOD in front of my morbid board of horrors and waited for the answer to jump out at me. It never came, but a knock at my door did before it swung open and Heath stepped inside. I looked over my shoulder to see that he had coffee and food in his hands before he set it down beside my bed.

"For you, my love," he said, handing over a coffee cup.

"Thank you."

My cheeks blushed at his endearment, but I'd lie and say it was the heat from the cup before I admitted that to him. Though, I knew he knew. He always knew. I took a sip and looked over to see him watching me. I wondered if this would be another still he'd immortalize onto paper. It baffled me that someone could be so infatuated with me. So obsessed with my presence . . .

I loved it.

"What have you come up with?" He diverted his attention back to the board, and I caught the flush of his cheeks. *Surely his is from the heat of the coffee as well*, I thought to myself and chuckled. He looked at me, and I cleared my throat.

"Sorry, um, nothing?" I gave him an awkward grin. "There's no rhyme or reason to anything we've discovered. We know the likely motive is money regarding Aspendale, but why the interns? What's the reason for killing off several people one by one in the oddest increments?"

"We know Aspendale was the first death. If they're all connected, then there's a trigger somewhere."

"How do we find it without the motive and culprit?" I asked him.

"Aspendale." I waited for him to elaborate. There was nothing helpful downstairs. "We draw out Aspendale and demand straightforward answers. No more riddles and guessing games."

"That's fine and all, but I'm sure it's an unspoken rule that ghosts can only talk in riddles and clues because we tried that before. He just repeated his cryptic messages." I sighed, looking at the faces again and again. "Besides, without using the journal, how do we draw him out?"

"You dreamed of him last time, so maybe we connect with him there again."

"I'm not in charge of that," I reminded him.

"I know, but it's worth a shot." He wasn't wrong, ambitious and misguided but not entirely wrong.

"When do you think we'll see another intern gone? We're down to four."

"I don't know, but entertain a thought?"

"I'm listening," I said, encouraging him.

"Let's track when Aspendale started making himself known and his visits to you."

"You think there's a clue?"

"It can't just a be a coincidence."

I wrote down the list of dates and what happened with each encounter. Slowly, the timeline started to fill out. The journey of my haunting transformed from malevolent. Aspendale was desperate—

there was no other way around it. I could forgive the violence knowing what we did now.

"We're due for a visit," Heath said as I pinned the last encounter to the wall.

"We're due for a death."

SEVENTEEN
THE HAUNTING OF BLAIR GRIMM

BLAIR

SLEEP WAS UNEVENTFUL. I tossed and turned until I gave up and sat in the bed, looking out into the room. Everything had been so heavy on my mind that it kept me from the one thing I needed to do in order to possibly connect with Aspendale again.

I had half a mind to text Heath and see if he was awake. He'd said he was going to research ways to contact spirits and I'd promised to sleep. Leaving my phone where it was, I got up and walked to my bathroom. My suite door rattled. I turned, expecting Heath, but saw nothing.

"Heath?" I called out into the empty room. No response came. I turned toward the bathroom, and the door rattled again. "Aspendale? If it's you, please show yourself." I felt silly talking to nothing, like those ghost hunting people on TV walking around, shouting demands like weirdos.

I approached the door with caution, hoping it wouldn't fly open. The rattling had stopped, so ever so carefully, I turned the handle. A gust of air met me and a scream pierced through the night. I ran into Heath's room, not caring if he was awake or asleep. It was dark, and I ran into the bedpost before reaching his bedside.

"Wha', huh?" he mumbled in the dark. I crawled into his bed and held onto him. "Blair?" he said, more awake now.

"It's happening again. Aspendale is somewhere and someone is dying." Heath turned on a lamp and rubbed his eyes.

"Where is—" he started but stopped and stared off at a corner of his room. "Never mind."

"What does he want?" I whispered to Heath.

"What do you want?" he echoed.

"Find the pieces. Another death. Find the pieces."

The ghostly voice that was becoming far too

familiar filled the dead space in the room. He repeated this over and over. I slapped my hands over my ears. The night was filled with screams and demands. Death and discovery. I couldn't take it anymore.

"Stop it. Stop it. Stop it," I whispered over and over.

"Blair," Heath said, pulling my hands away from my ears. "It's over, but we have another clue. He said 'Find the buried and free the damned,' and I think that means the graveyard."

"If not, that's a lot of land to cover. Do we go tonight? I don't want another visit like that."

"No," he assured me. "We can locate the potential areas tomorrow during the day and dig them up at night. You need rest. You look tired." Heath kissed my forehead and tucked me into his side.

"What are we supposed to do with all of these pieces?" I asked as he turned the lamp off.

"I wish I knew. Outside of the obvious answer, I hope it leads us to a clue regarding who's behind all of this."

The darkness was calm and still. I enjoyed its silence, the only sound Heath's heartbeat against my ear.

"At the very least, I'd like my suspicions confirmed."

"What are those?" I whispered, scared that speaking too loudly would cause the night to roar to life again.

"In due time, little one. In due time. Sleep."

EIGHTEEN
THE GRAVEYARD GHOUL

BLAIR

THIS IS SO MORBID, I thought to myself as Heath and I walked through the graveyard. It was surprisingly large considering the size of the property. A light drizzle set in, and I was thankful for the umbrella Heath had had the forethought to pack in his bag.

I broke the silence we'd been walking in.

"Has anything caught your eye?"

"Other than the most beautiful woman in the world walking by my side? No, not yet." He grinned, proud of himself, and much to my chagrin, I blushed at the statement. Heath was charming, and he'd maintained that charm. It was easy to fall into.

"What should we be looking for?"

"Freshly disturbed dirt is the only thing I can think of that would be obvious. There hasn't been a burial on the property in ages, so there shouldn't be any recent graves."

As we walked along, we fell back into a comfortable silence. The only sounds were the wet ground squishing beneath our feet and the pitter patter of light raindrops on the umbrella. Heath's knuckles brushed the back of my hand, and soon he slipped his fingers between mine.

My face burned. I was a grown woman blushing over a man holding my hand. He touched me so gently and with the utmost care. It was hard to imagine a better love after this thing with him. Was it only a thing?

It doesn't have to be, I thought. There were no rules about this sort of thing. We were adults, colleagues at best. *Would he want that?* I looked up at him, shadowed by the umbrella's arched cover. He smiled at me, a casual and peaceful grin. *Yes,* I told myself. *He would want this.*

"My love, what are you staring at?" His mouth

moved and the words caught up to me afterward, breaking the spell he continued to put me under.

"I was . . . I was caught up in thoughts about you."

"That's sweet. Care to share any of them?" I looked to the ground and away from his piercing gaze.

"No, thank you."

"Little crow—"

He'd been teasing me but stopped short and halted. A step ahead of him, I looked over my shoulder and caught his distress.

"What is it?"

"A few rows over, do you see him?" I scanned the grounds, sighting the ghostly figure watching us.

"Aspendale sure has a way with hints," I muttered to myself. It got a chuckle from Heath.

"This is by far the most interesting haunting I've ever experienced." We started walking toward the grave that Aspendale stood at.

"There have been others?" I asked, genuinely curious about his stories.

"Plenty, and I can't wait to share them all with you," he said as we turned onto the row.

"Would you look at that," I said, pointing to the first headstone at Aspendale's feet. The ground was loose and in a mound-like shape unlike the other graves around it. "I stand by the fact that we would've found it on our own."

"We would have. This is obvious." After a beat he added, "Almost too obvious."

"Please," Aspendale begged. Heath adjusted our umbrella to hide our conversation from outside eyes.

"Who did this to you?" he asked.

"Please," Aspendale repeated himself.

"We're coming back tonight," I said, gently reasoning with an entity incapable of reason. His face set with anger in his brows. There was a sudden wave of exhaustion over my body and I relaxed into Heath. His arm wrapped around me and he held me up.

"Stop that!" Heath yelled, and the pressing weight of exhaustion left me.

"You said you'd help me, move faster. More will die." Aspendale vanished afterward.

Heath sighed and repositioned our umbrella as droplets snuck past its barrier. He watched me as I stood on my own and let my energy restore.

"We'll come back tonight. I don't care how grumpy my grandfather gets. He'll get over it. He has all eternity." Heath chuckled at that and kissed my temple.

"Does the grave sound important?" I looked at the name and dates, but nothing came to the forefront right away.

"Not right now. What about for you?" I asked him.

"I didn't see any case files for this person. It's still likely this was a patient who died on the property and their family didn't want anything to do with them. I'll go through those records before we come back without drawing too much suspicion." Heath moved closer to me as the frigid breeze became a gust.

"The haunting was already a lot, but now I feel like a grave robber. I hate this."

HEATH

Darkness had fallen and we stood at the grave of Eleanor Roberts once again. I looked at the manor; it was dark and I saw no movement in the corridors by us.

"Eleanor Roberts," I started, sticking my shovel in the ground and heaving out dirt. "She wasn't a patient, at least not by the records I found. I'd say she was a family member or distant relative."

"Do you think it's buried deep?" I shoveled more.

"Doubtful." Another heap of dirt landed to my left. "I have my suspicions, and I don't see them digging six feet down in the night." Just as I said that, a piece of cloth came through the soil. I dropped the shovel and got down on my knees. I moved the dirt with my hands, finding ripped pieces of paper mixed in.

When I uncovered the cloth bundle, it didn't take long to confirm the missing limbs of Aspendale. I grabbed a few pieces of paper and tried to discern what they could've been a part of.

"This looks like numbers? Maybe an expense report? I'm not sure, but it's finance related for sure." Dirt smeared too much to determine more.

"So, money continues to be the motive."

NINETEEN
WICKED AS THEY COME

NORMAN ASPENDALE

I don't really know where to start with this entry. It serves no purpose other than a record of my discovery should anything happen to me. Someone will surely find everything.

I worry about Cressida, or more to the fact I worry for my legacy should Blair not wish to take the estate and all I leave to her. As it stands, Cressida wants it all and she's proven she'll stop at nothing to obtain it.

Today, I discovered the paper trail that shows Cressida has falsified reports and skewed data points. If it was a means to look better with her patients and contracts, well, there's no way to make the wicked desirable. I want to investigate her, but I haven't found the proper means to do so. It's a rather daunting task and I'd need help, but I'm not sure who I can trust in the manor and who might be on her side. Not that there even are sides, but money and threats will create them fast.

Just today, she pressed me again to reopen the asylum. To step away from our forensic contracts and embrace the legacy.

I never saw it as a legacy. I saw it as a stain. The barbaric psychiatry that came of that name was no future of mine. It wouldn't be a future I'd hand to Blair, either.

If I could hire two interns, I do believe I'd be able to leverage all that I needed to weed her monstrosity from this practice.

I've come to the solution. There will be an apprenticeship or internship of sorts. A group I'll narrow down over time that will work on uncovering and correcting Cressida's mistakes. She won't know what I'm really up to until it's all been collected and evaluated. I'll just let her go and part ways with her. It's simple, foolproof. I'll bring Blair here. Surely her interest in my practice when I was at her university will entice her to apply. If I start the process now, by the end of the year, we can be free of Cressida without repercussions. I fear what she will do. What she's capable of. She hid it well in her interviews and early years of working in my practice, but I see the psychological disturbances within her. I just hope I can keep her under control for a little while longer. Just long enough to bring in more help that she can't gain control over.

Cressida's outbursts have increased and her behavior is erratic. I fear I won't be able to meet Blair and explain our complicated family. I feel my days are growing shorter and shorter. The internship starts soon and I've sent out Blair's acceptance, but I fear it won't be me who gets to greet my granddaughter. I worry for her. All that I've heard about her speaks to a strength and intelligence that's to be admired. I worry still.

This was a bad idea. It was a fool's plan. I have failed Blair.

TWENTY
HIS LITTLE CROW

BLAIR

HEATH STAYED quiet as we snuck our way through the manor and across the grounds. He walked me toward the asylum. The moon was obstructed by clouds, and the building was hard to make out in the pitch black.

"Heath? What are we doing here?" I whispered, looking over my shoulder in fear of being caught where we shouldn't be.

"I'll show you," he said, moving us up the steps and into the receiving room of the asylum. The door creaked as he closed it behind us. "Have you ever wanted to do, to be, so depraved?"

"Heath . . ."

"You drive me mad, little crow. I want to show you just how mad you make me." He took my hand, and I was stunned into silence. We walked into a large room with grand windows. I leaned back against a table. An eerie feeling set in as I peered outside. It felt like we were being watched.

Heath moved in front of me and obstructed my view. His fingers moved over my blouse, unbuttoning the garment with speed. I looked up at him and gripped the edge of the table. Gone was the kind, patient man I'd come to know. In his place was someone hungry and desperate. Heath looked crazed as he warred with himself. His gentleness faltered and a couple of buttons ripped and popped against the floor.

"I'm sorry," he forced out. He moved closer, breath hot against my skin as he kissed and licked over my exposed flesh.

"It's okay," I whispered. I reached out for him, but he stopped me. His grip was tight around my wrist.

"Blair," he started, using the last of his composure. "I care about you—more than I should right now."

"Okay," I managed to say. I cared about him, too,

but I couldn't focus on anything more than the press of Heath's cock against me.

"I want you to remember that."

"W-why?" I stammered out as he unzipped my skirt and it fell around my ankles. His hands roved over my body with a touch just shy of being rough. He dropped to a knee, pulling down my lacy underwear as he went. He kissed up my thighs before swiping his tongue through my center.

"Because with your permission, I'm going to hurt you tonight."

He kissed and licked at my pussy. My fingers dove into his silky hair. I held him to me as he feasted. Gentle fingers entered me before he fucked me hard. My weight mostly rested on the table as my legs quivered and started to give out.

"Heath," I cried out on a cresting orgasm. His fingers dug into the flesh of my thighs and ass. He wasn't going to let me go.

In one swift motion as I fell back against the tabletop, he picked me up. My legs rested on his shoulders, and I ached to touch him. When he looked up, his lips glistened with my cum. There was a new darkness in his eyes as he looked at me like I was prey.

Carefully, he lowered my legs and set them in a position that left me on display to him.

"Don't move," he said.

"Yes, sir."

I waited as he undid his belt and freed his cock. If we hadn't fucked before, I would've sworn he wouldn't fit. He pressed the tip against my entrance, and I desperately wanted him to take what he needed, however rough. I needed him inside me, and as he lazily stroked an inch or so deep, it drove me to insanity.

"Please," I begged him. "Please, Heath." He retreated, and I threw my head back in a desperate fit to have him. My hands hit the table and gripped the edge to keep from moving closer to him.

His cock speared me suddenly and without warning. I cried out as my chest arched and my back lifted off the table. I was deliciously full. There was nothing better than the feel of him rutting inside. His fingers dug into me so forcefully, his nails would leave tiny cuts on my skin.

A swift hand caught my throat, and a lightheadedness set in as he squeezed and squeezed. Movement caught my attention, and through blurred vision, I could've sworn Cressida stood in the window. The table groaned and squeaked as he fucked me stupid.

"My favorite brain," he said, lessening his grip on my throat. "My favorite heart. My favorite girl," he cooed. "Who do you belong to?" There was a sense of dizziness as he played with his grip around my throat.

"You," I slurred, fighting against the sensation of passing out.

"Who are you, Blair?" he asked, backing off the pressure just a bit more. My vision blurred. He fucked me hard and deep. I'd be anyone and anything for him.

"Your little crow," I whispered, and he released me.

"Good girl."

As my world righted and Heath pulled out, I chanced a look behind him but saw no one. *It's fine. No one's there. Get out of your head.*

"I want you on your knees, now."

"Yes, sir," I echoed. Moving to my hands and knees, I steadied my breath and heart rate. He kissed my backside before he swiped his tongue over my ass. A groan left me as I thought of every wicked thing I wanted him to do to me.

"Spread them, go lower." I did as he instructed,

and his hands met my hips as he held me in place. He rutted so deep inside me, it felt as though he were coming through my throat. I couldn't speak, could only hold on with each thrust that was sure to send me over the table's edge if I didn't.

I felt another orgasm crest as he angled his hips. No one had ever fucked me like this, and it felt so new and good. I screamed as I tightened around him. A flash of lightning followed by a crack of thunder came after. My cries were lost to the rain pelting the glass and the thunder rolling through the sky.

This was haunting.

"Blair," he whispered, pulling me up by my hair in a painful arch. Tears pricked at my eyes. "I need you with me," he started. I was there. My head spun, but I enjoyed the feeling. "I want to hurt you. How dark are you willing to go with me?" He pulled my hair back, and the pain sent a shiver over my body. My nipples peaked.

"I like pain, hurt me, Heath."

"I want to cut you," he said, cradling me into his chest. The faintest expression of gentleness in his touch.

"Yes."

TWENTY-ONE
HER DARK LOVE

HEATH

YES. *Yes. Yes.* She said yes. It was unexpected. Blair didn't seem to be the type to want to play with knives, and I was afraid of scaring her off.

"They're just going to be shallow cuts," I said, talking her through it as I worked my cock inside her. "It'll sting like a paper cut. I won't hurt you," I promised her. Time and time again, I'd thought about doing this to her. Hoping she'd say yes. Her skin was too pretty and unmarred. I wanted to mark her as mine.

I pulled her close to me, feeling the way she squeezed my cock.

"Don't move," I whispered in her ear. She was breathing hard, and I held her delicately by the throat. I pulled the knife from my pocket and flipped the blade out. "Shallow cuts," I reminded her.

I ran the knife over her thigh, and she whimpered before relaxing into me. Tiny rivulets ran down her leg.

"You're doing so good, little crow."

I made another cut and she moaned. "Heath," she breathed out, her head dropping back into my chest.

The third cut made the rivulets run thicker.

"Shh, bleed for me, love." Her blood stained my hand as I squeezed her thigh.

"Yes, sir."

I made matching cuts on her other thigh, and through it all, she sat still for me. I licked the blade clean and put it away.

"Down," I ordered.

"Yes, sir." She bent over, slipping off my cock and putting her ass in the air for me.

"Do you need me to stop?"

"No, sir." My hand flew through the air and smacked her ass hard enough to welt the flesh. She said nothing, zoned out and in her space.

"Safeword if you need to and I'll stop immediately."

"Yes, sir."

I ran my hands over her thighs, squeezing as she continued to bleed for me. It coated my hands, and I stroked my cock. I slipped two fingers into her pussy. Her ass moved back and followed my touch.

"Greedy little cunt." I grabbed her hips and thrust into her. I bottomed out, and she held onto the table with a white-knuckled grip. She met each punishing snap of my hips. I leaned over and bit her shoulder hard enough to bruise and draw blood. I did it again and again. She screamed as her release flooded the space between us and soaked the table.

"Come for me, Blair. Only for me."

"Yes, sir," she cried, sprawled on the table. I pinned her wrists and rutted into her. I wanted to live inside her. Feel her around me constantly. Grabbing the back of her neck, I angled deeper, and she started to tremble beneath me.

"Let go, love." She struggled under my grasp. "I have you, let go."

A bloodcurdling scream left her as she squirted and squirmed. I fucked her harder and harder, covering her mouth with my other hand.

"Scream all you want; fight me, Blair. You're not

getting free." I grunted, feeling the electricity move down my spine. "Fuck, fuck, fuck." My hips jerked as I tried to delay it. "I'm coming, love . . ."

My release hit hard, taking my breath and making me see stars as we collapsed on the table. I wrapped Blair into me. She wasn't getting free, not now . . . not ever. She was mine.

I pushed myself off the table and adjusted my clothes. We were a sticky, wonderful mess. She lay unmoving. I grabbed her chin and shook her head gently, snapping my fingers to get her attention.

"Love." She grunted in response, and that was good enough for now. "I'm going to take you back," I whispered to her. I dressed her as best as I could as she lay there lifeless and spent. Gathering her in my arms, I walked out of the asylum and headed straight for her room.

I undressed Blair as she whined and whimpered. Her eyes were still closed, and she went back and forth between sleeping and wakefulness.

"The bath is ready," I whispered, and she grunted. I chuckled and stood with her in my arms, carefully stepping into the steaming tub. "The cuts will sting at first." I continued to talk her through it before I sat down and submerged us both.

"Ow, ow," she cried out, waking up a little more and looking around us.

"I warned you," I said, kissing her hand. "It'll stop hurting soon. Lie back with me. Let me clean and take care of you."

The clear water turned pink as I scrubbed the dried blood from our skin. Blair went back to sleep on my chest. This was the most content I'd felt in a long time. My heart beat harder. Blair was becoming the most important person in my life. My care for her was evolving daily.

I could fall for her.

I would, in fact.

She was inevitable.

TWENTY-TWO
CAT'S OUT OF THE BAG

BLAIR

MY BODY WAS stiff in the morning, and I opted for my flats over heels to make walking more comfortable. Waking up with Heath had been a delight, but more so being taken care of like he had done was something entirely new. All morning, he doted on me and checked in on how I felt. It was refreshing.

Today was another round in Aspendale's office, and we'd been careful to avoid Cressida's suspicion. Death after death, there was no doubt anymore. Heath hadn't said it, but he thought it, surely. I'd come to the conclusion after reading the journal yesterday.

Heath sat in Aspendale's office chair, reading through documents.

"Can I just voice something crazy?" Heath looked up at me and nodded slowly. "Cressida is behind all of this, right? That's what all the clues are building up to?"

"I've come to the same conclusion," Heath confirmed. "But, we don't have anything beyond circumstantial evidence, if we even have that."

"The journal—"

"Is a great place to start, little crow. We're on the right path at the very least. We'll catch her in the act and call the police, problem solved."

"That simple?" I asked, crossing the room.

"That simple."

I wanted to believe him. He sorted papers on Aspendale's desk into piles for patient records, financial documents, and data that'd been altered.

"Stop," he said abruptly. He looked down at my feet.

"What is it?"

"You aren't wearing heels today so I almost didn't hear it. Walk back over there and then come back toward the desk, please." I backtracked and did as he asked. "There!" He shot up out of the chair and came over, knocking over the wood until the sound changed. "It's different here."

He worked to slip the boards apart, revealing a hidden compartment in the floor.

"Is that blood?" I asked, peering over his shoulder.

"It looks like it." Inside the floor was clothing with dark stains.

"You think these belonged to Aspendale? He was in the morgue and everyone else was found dressed."

"It makes sense," Heath said, careful to look and not touch. My heart beat loudly and panic surged inside me. He put the boards back in place and opened his mouth but stopped.

"What is it?" I whispered.

"We aren't alone," he said quietly. "Behind the desk, go." I stood and ran to the desk, and he followed, quickly gathering the papers and dropping them into a desk drawer. He sat in the chair and undid his pants. "On your knees, fast."

I dropped to my knees, and he wrapped my hair around his hand.

"Heath—"

"Trust me and start blowing me."

"Excuse me?" I heard it then, the footsteps outside, followed by the turn of the door handle. I quickly took him in my mouth and moved my head up and down.

"Fuck, Blair, I didn't think—fuck." He moaned. I looked up to see his cheeks reddening. The door swung open as Heath dropped his head back. We scrambled apart as Cressida cleared her throat.

"Keep these acts private to your quarters," she started, looking us up and down. "Or the asylum."

The last part chilled me. She had been there last night.

"I'm sorry," Heath started. "We were doing work and wanted a quiet place to fool around. This is my fault," he said, putting his clothes back together and reaching for me. We stood, and he guided me through the room and past Cressida. Her eyes moved up and down my body.

"I better not catch you in here again."

"Yes, ma'am," Heath and I said in unison. Down the hall and out of earshot, Heath pulled me in close.

"We're going back in there tonight," he whispered.

After avoiding Cressida's judgment for the day, we dressed down in all black and crept around the manor to avoid the staff as we made our way back to Aspendale's office. Heath tried the doorknob, and it was still unlocked. We slipped inside without a sound and went back to the desk to go over the paperwork. Heath pulled out his flashlight and started reading.

"I recognize a name here," he whispered. "It was on one of my assignments."

"Do you think there's a correlation?"

"We need his original list for each intern. Start in the filing cabinets," he instructed. As quietly as possible, we started rifling through his files. He was a meticulous man, so there had to be a copy for Cressida to have followed up until now.

"I think I found them, look." Heath handed me a file folder, and I flipped through it. Sure enough, there were the plans for each intern.

"I've seen this name in the financial files."

"Yes, you have. All of these names are corresponding files with Cressida's malpractice." He looked between two files and then back to me. "We need to murder board this one."

TWENTY-THREE
THE DEVIL HERSELF

BLAIR

WE SMUGGLED the paperwork back to my suite and started matching the files to the interns. The man who'd gone missing initially had a task directly under Cressida. Day by day, Cressida had picked off the interns who were getting too close to her or had already uncovered her questionable work.

"Something isn't sitting right with me," I said as I pinned the last document under the most recent intern to die.

"What's that, love?"

"Why go through all of this?" I stared at our work in disbelief. "We know her motives, but why not just kill Aspendale, cancel the internship, and forge his will?"

"Serial killers aren't my specialty, but have you considered the fact that maybe she's so sick and twisted that she wanted this to be a game for her?" His words were chilling and I didn't want to rationalize such a deplorable human being's motive.

"Switching to another morbid thought process, do you think we can predict who she kills next?"

"Well," he started, standing and walking over to the murder board. "I think we're safe for now because we haven't been doing any work. Should that not be the case, I'd go before you in her eyes."

"Why is that?" I asked, confused on why I wouldn't be a prime target for her.

"You are special to this estate, yes. However." He turned to face me. "Greater torture comes from watching everyone around you die, leaving you helpless."

"That's fucking terrible."

"I know, love. So, let's say we're last given we haven't done anything. That leaves this intern." Heath reached over and tapped the girl's photo. Vivienne Sinclair.

"Why hasn't she left?"

"Why haven't we left?"

"I see your point, but what reason is there to stay?"

"Why do you think she's *able* to leave?" he asked casually.

"What's stopping her?"

"Fear is the easy answer," he said. "Maybe someone told her they were leaving only to die the next day. It's been what, only a week or just a little more and we're down to three interns. How much of that time has she spent on planning to leave?"

"That's fair," I conceded. "I can't believe Aspendale thought this was the way to fix this."

"Personally, I feel like he thought you'd be able to uncover it."

"I'd have rather not lived it." I sighed. This was becoming frustrating. "You know what? This is silly. I'm not a detective or a superhero. I say we just call the police, report a suspicious death, and then we're done with it."

I pulled out my phone and walked across the room while dialing 9-1-1. The call connected and rang once. Twice.

By the fourth ring, my confidence dropped into a frown.

"What's wrong?"

"It's just ringing."

"Did you dial it right?" he teased. I rolled my eyes.

"Of course I dialed it right, Heath. I just don't understand. It's an endless ring. A voicemail would've clicked on by now or even a disconnected tone. There's just a ring." I pulled the phone away from my ear and looked down.

There was no service.

"That's weird," I mused out loud.

"What's that?"

"Pull out your phone please," I said, crossing the room and looking down at his screen. No service. "When did we lose our cell service? Can she block 9-1-1?"

"It's possible," he said, sighing and pocketing his phone. "Without knowing anything for certain, let's operate as though these are useless and we're alone. How are we stopping her?"

"*Can* we stop her?" I asked. It felt like a losing battle. There were three of us left and anyone was up for grabs.

"I don't know that we can right now, but I'd be willing to try. First, we need concrete proof it's Cressida. If my guess is correct, we're last to go. Let's stake out Vivienne's room later."

"Would she strike tonight?"

"It's been a couple of days," he reminded me. "If she's this deep in, it's probably eating her up that she hasn't killed anyone in such a long time."

"Okay, tonight then. We get our proof, but then what?"

"We can try the police again, but I guarantee the emergency numbers are all blocked."

What he said sent terror through me. We were trapped in this house with a killer and no way out. Presumed killer, but it made sense. I paced back and forth, thinking it over.

"Vivienne is in our wing. How should we do this?"

"Well," he said, "there are a couple of options. We can either go and hide in the stairwell or we can use the empty suite on the second floor."

"Empty suite," I confirmed. I wanted to catch her in the act.

THE NIGHT CAME SLOWLY. My anxiety was on overdrive as we waited in the empty suite. Vivienne was a fellow east-wing resident who stayed on the second floor. Getting past her room unnoticed was easy enough, but there was no telling what Cressida would notice. Or do, for that matter. This was completely based on chance and a few hunches. I trusted Heath's gut instinct that it was her, but I wanted it to be wrong. Vivienne had been a perfect candidate, should it have been a real and fair shot. We'd been brought here to our demises unknowingly, and I struggled with that knowledge of my grandfather's actions. Though his heart had been in a good place and he'd been in need of help, it weighed heavy on mind that so many had died because of his choices.

Was it cowardice? I couldn't say that faced with the same decision, I would've made a better plan, but surely there had to have been one. Though, it was clear that Cressida had pull in more places than just the manor.

"Blair," Heath whispered to me, breaking up my rambling thoughts and pulling me back to the present task at hand.

"Yes?"

"Your mind is racing, you haven't said a word in thirty minutes. What's going on?"

"Nothing," I said, brushing him off. "It's not going to help us right now."

"Well, I'm here if you need to talk about anything." I looked up at him. His smile was kind and genuine. His hair was messy today, half-done after his shower, and he looked delicious. His chest was exposed in his dress shirt. I noticed he favored unbuttoning the top, and it was my favorite look on him.

We were opposites in a few ways, but style was the main feature. He was the light to my darkness.

"You look like you want to eat me," he said, bringing my attention away from his body and back to him.

"I do," I started. "But given the circumstances . . ."

"Best to not be caught during a potential murder." I nodded. The gravity of the situation started to weigh on me. "Hey, stay with me. Don't get lost in thoughts again. It'll be okay."

"You have such high hopes."

"I've always been more optimistic than most." I smiled at that. I admired his optimism, but the reality was too damning to ignore. If this went wrong, a single misstep, we were dead.

Heath looked at his watch, and I peeked through the cracked door. We decided that it wouldn't be enough to notice, but I doubted that heavily.

It'd been dark for some time now, and the noise

in Vivienne's suite had died down. She was probably asleep.

The sound of heels on hardwood floors made my spine straighten. Cressida. Heath and I looked at each other and nodded. It was time.

They grew louder before stopping. The sound of a key sliding into the lock caught my attention. Because of course she would have a master key to the rooms. I questioned all the times I'd come back to my room unlocked in that moment. I'd been blaming the ghost, but what if it had been Cressida trying to come after me or catch me with my guard down?

I couldn't ask Heath now, but if we made it out of this . . .

A door creaked and my breath stilled. I couldn't see anything through the crack in the door; it was too dark and she was too far away. My heartbeat pounded in my chest. One, two, three—

A scream pierced the air and my breath hitched. Gurgles followed, and I looked at Heath just as Aspendale materialized behind him. I went to speak, but Heath grabbed me and covered my mouth with his hand as he ushered me into the closet. He kept me close and didn't remove his hand. My chest pounded in time with Cressida's steps as they grew closer to the room.

Our door creaked open more, and I could see her through the slats. She turned in the moonlight and blood spatter colored her white blouse. *Vivienne's dead. We're going to die.*

Heath held me tighter, and I wanted to whimper. It started to hurt. *We can't stop her. She's going to kill us next.*

A loud clatter came from the direction of the stairwell and she turned.

"Damn brats," she muttered before marching out of the room. When her footsteps faded, Heath released me.

My breath came out in heavy pants.

"It's okay—"

"Vivienne is dead," I hissed. "Nothing is okay." Heath's hands wrapped around my arms.

"Call me callous or cruel, I don't care. So long as you are alive, everything is okay for me." Heath opened the closet door and peered down the hall.

A breeze hit my back before I felt another energy drain. *Aspendale.* I turned to face my grandfather.

"Go, you only have minutes. I've led her away as best as I can." Heath took my hand and led me out as we ran back to his room.

We were sitting ducks.

TWENTY-FOUR
LAST TO SURVIVE

BLAIR

IN HEATH'S ROOM, I sat on his bed and started scrolling through search results on the internet. None of the interns' deaths had been reported and none of the interns had been deemed missing. We were alone. There was no news coverage, no police reports, and no one to rescue us.

I tried to dial out again, but it wouldn't connect. I searched for the internship, but it hadn't been publicized either. This had been the perfect plan. I paced Heath's room, but he watched me in silence.

"I'm going to call the police again." I stopped and

dialed 9-1-1, begging the universe for the tiniest bit of help. A dial tone rang out and then a dispatcher connected.

"9-1-1, what's your emergency?"

"Oh, thank god. There's been a series of murders at the Aspendale Manor. Several interns have died—"

"Ma'am, the manor has been closed for the last two months. You're the fifth prank call this week. It's illegal to waste our time, and I suggest you not call in again with your same scary stories."

"But it's not—"

"Find a new hobby," she said before disconnecting the line.

"What happened?" Heath asked, standing up.

"She didn't believe me. She said there were multiple prank calls and that I need a new hobby." I stared at my phone in disbelief. Heath's hand came into view as he took my phone and pocketed it before wrapping me up in a hug. "What do we do?" I cried into his shoulder.

"We survive and we take down Cressida. But first, we sleep. It's late and you need to rest."

"But Cressida has a master key. What's stopping her from coming up here and killing us?" Heath sighed as his arms tightened around me.

"I'll make sure that doesn't happen. Sleep, little crow."

TWENTY-FIVE
NO WAY OUT

HEATH

BLAIR SLEPT in my arms as I watched my door. I hadn't heard Cressida all night. Her distinct heel clicks on the hardwood never came, but I didn't sleep regardless.

It was one thing to assume she was the killer; it was another to be confronted with it in the most terrifying way. I wouldn't let Blair die in this house.

A sleepy noise came from beside me before Blair sat up.

"Good morning, love," I said gently. "How'd you sleep?" Her perfume swirled around me. It was my new favorite scent.

"Rough. Have you been awake for long?"

"I didn't sleep. I told you I'd make sure you were safe." She stared, her eyes bouncing between mine and starting to mist. A yawn escaped me before I could stop it, and her brows knitted together. "I'm fine, I promise."

"We need to stop her. Today."

"We will," I promised her.

"Why do you think she left us alone? She has to know we know something is going on."

"I assume she likes the thrill of theatrics."

Blair rolled out of bed and pulled on some comfy clothes of mine before tossing her voluminous hair into a big bun on her head. She was drop-dead gorgeous in her business attire, her looks were lethal, but this was when she was most beautiful to me. Dressed for comfort with her guard down was my favorite.

After I followed suit and grabbed another pair of sweats, we brushed our teeth and tried to go over a game plan to no avail. Cressida had all the advantage here.

"Maybe we hide out in Aspendale's office?" Blair offered.

"Either way we're sitting ducks. Let's avoid her path for now and go back to researching hard evidence." Blair nodded and followed behind me as I walked to my door.

Opening it, I had something to say, but words caught in my throat at the sight of what waited for us on the other side. Blair moved past me before I could stop her, halting her stride and looking up to face a demented and twisted Cressida. All of her teeth were on display in a wicked smile that chilled and froze me.

"I've been waiting for you," she hissed. Her hand flew across the space between us and she hit Blair in the nose. "And I've been waiting to do that ever since I laid eyes on you, bitch." Blood poured and stained my white T-shirt as Blair cried out in pain.

I didn't condone hitting women, but my fist flew out and connected with Cressida's face in a sickening crunch. She staggered back, holding her cheek, and I pulled Blair's arm and ran down the hall. We couldn't stay trapped with our backs against a wall.

"Are you okay?" I rushed out as we ran down the spiral staircase of the east wing.

"I'll be fine," she mumbled behind her hand.

At the annex, I looked over at Blair and we ran to the front door. I pulled as hard as I could, but it wouldn't budge. I tried everything to find a lock but there wasn't one—she'd locked us inside.

"This is why no one could just leave," I said, exasperated and completely out of ideas. We couldn't just take her on like this without a plan. She'd ambushed us. Heels clicked over hardwood, and we faced the annex. I pushed Blair behind me and her hands fisted the back of my shirt. "We can't stay here," I said, urging her toward the main hall.

Aspendale appeared in the hallway, and I took it as our only sign. I led us toward his office.

TWENTY-SIX
NO WAY BACK

BLAIR

HEATH PUSHED me into the office and locked the door behind us. Some good that would do since Cressida could come and go in the manor wherever she pleased. Panic surged through me. My heart raced and my face pounded with pressure. She'd broken my nose.

"Behind his desk, go. Now." I did as Heath instructed and waited there in silence. I eyed the letter opener and took it up as the only weapon I had. Heath came to my side and dropped to the floor.

He held me close, muttering apologies into my shoulder. I cried. This was it. This was how this good thing in my life would end, and no one would know. Not for a while at least. I didn't know if Heath had family waiting on him, but mine knew when I'd be back. Only, I wasn't coming back. We weren't coming back.

"Blair," he whispered, grabbing my face and pinning my stare to his. "I've fallen head over heels for you. You were the greatest and brightest thing to have happened to me and my only regret is how this will end. I'm so sorry I couldn't stop this."

"It's not your fault," I whispered, kissing him sweetly. Our last kiss. Our last touch.

Just then the door flung open, banging against the wall. I jumped. He pushed me into the cubby space under the desk and held up his hand for me to stay put. He stood.

I wanted to cry out for him to stop, to stay with me. It would've done no good.

"Where's the bitch?" Cressida hissed. Heath said nothing, and she laughed like a lunatic. "You can't protect her, Mr. Crowley. I've savored this—waited for so long. I preemptively tried to kill you, but this timeline worked much better. You were too alert before. Ghosts and ghouls filled your mind then."

"Shut up," he said as he moved back. I tucked myself into the cubby tighter as her heels clicked across the floor and she came around the desk, backing him into the main space.

Her heels moved around the other end—he was drawing her away from me. I couldn't let him be alone with her. I couldn't lose him, not like this.

"You two have been a pain in my ass, but finally I can cut you down to nothing. I thought about killing you both while you fucked her in the asylum." I moved, peeking over the desk. "Where is she, Heath? I won't let her have that fortune. This is mine!"

They were against the wall of frames, and Heath's hand moved up to the one that covered the safe. She kept going on about what she'd do to me. He moved quickly, throwing open the frame and smacking her in the face with it.

She screamed and staggered back, clutching her already broken nose.

"You fucking bitch! I'm going to enjoy ripping you shreds and carving up your little whore!"

I was moving on autopilot with no other thought in my mind other than stopping her. I swung and plunged the letter opener into her throat from behind. Blood sprayed Heath as I removed it and stabbed again.

And again.

And again.

I wanted her to stop. I wanted this nightmare to end. She fell to the floor clutching her neck and gurgled and choked on blood. No words came out, and I raised the fisted letter opener again, but something caught my hand on my downward strike.

Heath.

"It's over, little crow. It's over, you can stop." Adrenaline filled me and urged me to keep going. I had to be sure. I had to know. "Baby, please. Look at me."

I did. His face was calm, no trace of fear marring his beautiful features. It was over.

He swept me into his arms, and we stayed like that for the longest time. Minutes passed, and finally I broke.

"It's over."

TWENTY-SEVEN
A NEW BEGINNING - EIGHT MONTHS LATER

HEATH

"MY LOVE," I said gently as I walked into the office. Blair sat on the floor, surrounded by files. "You've been at this all day."

"If I'm to have the practice back in full swing, I have to get this ready. I've got so many people breathing down my neck while cleaning up this mess." She didn't look up from the paperwork.

"Little crow," I whispered, and her head snapped up. "You have all the time in the world to get this place back in shape. Come be with me tonight." She looked behind her out the window and her eyebrows rose.

"I didn't realize the time."

"That's okay," I promised her.

It *was* okay. She was determined to bring this place back to life in the best ways. She wanted to maintain Aspendale's contracts and remodel the asylum for clinical services. It was going to take time, but she was headstrong and determined.

"We could also plan other things," I said, leaning against the doorframe.

"Like what?"

"Like a wedding..."

She laughed. "You haven't even proposed. That'd be a little premature." I shrugged my shoulders.

"Come with me." She looked around the room. "With me, little crow."

"Yes, sir." Blair stood up and stepped over the piles of paper carefully before taking my hand. "Where are we going?"

"It's a surprise." I walked her through the grounds and out to the greenhouse on the property. Blair insisted it be maintained, and the growth of late was beautiful. I found her out here most days, relaxing.

She took a deep breath when we stepped inside, and it didn't take long for her to start wandering around. I stayed a step behind her and waited. When she turned the corner and saw the white-and-black roses, she froze.

"When did those get in here?" she asked, running up to smell them. Behind her, I dropped to one knee and bided my time.

"Who knows . . ." She turned around at my casual tone just as I slid the ring box from my pocket.

"Oh my fuck," she exclaimed, and I laughed.

"Ms. Grimm, you are a delight unknown by many and I pity them. You are everything I've searched for, and yet there's still so much to be discovered. It would be an honor to spend the rest of my life with you. Will you marry me?" I opened the ring box as tears streamed down her face.

"Heath, I . . ." Her hand moved to her chest as she took big breaths. "I thought . . ." She scrambled for words and shook her head. A smile crept over her face. "Yes, of course!" She fell into my arms with sobs. "I thought you were joking about the wedding."

"No, baby." I smoothed my hand over her hair and held her close.

"I love you," she said, squeezing me tighter.

"I love you, too, Mrs. Crowley."

"No." She laughed. A grin pulled at the corner of

my mouth. We'd had this talk once before. "My last name is cooler."

"Grimm-Crowley." She pulled back and her makeup had run, probably staining my white dress shirt. "I'm so in love with you, Mrs. Grimm-Crowley." I took her face in my hands, kissing her softly as the salty tingle of tears crossed my tongue. "You're mine forever, little crow."

THE END

ACKNOWLEDGMENTS

I want to say thank you to my readers. You are the reason I write, even when it's hard.

To N.B., thank you for always pushing me and supporting my dreams as they change and take shape.

To Stacy, thank you for everything you do for me I wouldn't be here without you.

To Ethan, thank you for always having my back and telling me I would finish this. I finished it. I did it.

To my beta readers, you mean the world to me. Thank you for validating the story and giving it a chance.

ARC readers, you did the damn thing—thank you.

Patreon, without your support I couldn't keep writing. Thank you of everything you provide. You guys are amazing.

ABOUT THE AUTHOR

Kenna is pursuing far too many things all at once, but she wouldn't have the chaos any other way. She's a home favorite on Tiktok, the best ARC reader (okay, made that one up), and going mad figuring out her Master's degree. She became a hit on Tiktok after announcing to the world her love of Why Choose, and really it's only become more chaotic. Her mother's background in English planted the seed for writing and literature. (Sorry Mama B, she just reads smut now!) She's enjoyed books since she was in elementary school, and vividly remembers the carefree afternoons spent in her mother's school library. Shout out to Mrs. C for letting her take home books even though she wasn't a student yet! (And Kenna assures, the inspiration for the librarian in He Who Haunts Me was NOT you!) However, Ms. F, taking her Maximum Ride book in 6th grade (gifted by Gramma) was totally not f'n cool.

ALSO BY KENNA BELLRAE

He Who Haunts Me (Swallow's Archive Duet Book 1)

Dead Man's Wish (Swallow's Archive Duet Book 2)

All Hallows' Haunt (Hallows' Eve Hookups Book 1)

All Hallows' Hex (Hallows' Eve Hookups Book 2)

All Hallows' Rage (Hallows' Eve Hookups Book 3)

All Hallows Maze (Hallows' Eve Hookups Book 4)

Kisses From Cupid (Voracious Valentines Book 1)

CONNECT WITH KENNA BELLRAE

Instagram: novels_and_novellas
Facebook: Author Kenna Bellrae
Tiktok: asteamyromancenovel
Website: https://www.authorkennabellrae.com

Made in the USA
Monee, IL
08 December 2024